MELISSA
COBB

DO MY HEART A FAVOR

DO MY HEART
FAVOR

MELISSA COBB

PUBLISHER'S NOTE
This book is a work of fiction. Names, characters, businesses, Organization, places, events, and incidents are the product of the Author's imagination or are used fictionally. Any resemblance of Actual persons, living or dead, events, or locales are entirely coincidental.

Library of Congress Control Number: 201794678

ISBN 979-8-9931887-6-8

Published in United States

Dedication Page

"The Voice of Reason"

For those in need of someone to confide in, find your voice of reason. Allow the voice of reason to help make you a better person and to become full circle of the goals you wish to carry out. The voice of reason is the unbiased voice of you and your circumstances, for it will tell you the truth even if you don't want to hear it or like it (now that's friend).

As you listen to your voice of reason, don't forget the lessons and storms life has taught you as you make your move. Learn to listen to you if something does not feel right. In the process, love yourself a lot more, stress even less, laugh daily, cry when you are not sad, don't forget where you have been, be thankful for where you are going and be grateful, where you are at in your life; therefore, believe in REAL LOVE for it still exists because GOD IS LOVE.

CHAPTER 1

Marilyn the four-year-old, whom I called Lyn-clung-to-my-leg and Rosalyn the two-year-old, whom I call Rossi-cried-on-my-hip as their father, Cedric, frantically threw his clothes in his suitcase at dusk dark, for some reason. I stood there, wondering what was happening. He came home and told me he had had enough of not having what we needed. I completely understood, but why do I feel like I was the blame? As he picked up this and that, I followed him around with the children attached to me.

My husband of three years didn't talk to me much and for him to come in and walk past us, wasn't odd. He hadn't really said anything other than he was fed up and disgusted. I kept asking what the problem was, but he would not speak. As he continued getting all his things, he continued to ignore me. When he found the clothes, he was looking for he stopped in front of me. My heart escalated and was about to jump out my chest from the ripping effect of what could be.

Cedric for a few seconds rolled his eyes around the room as he spoke with no compassion or sympathy, "I'm tired of coming to this house and seeing you feeding babies or changing diapers. You never get dressed up and you never do anything I like to do. You are always too busy for me and my needs. I am in this by myself, and it is time for me to act like I am by myself. I don't need you and I damn sure don't want you anymore. I've found someone that laughs with me and

has time for me. We get along and Emma and I are on the same level because we understand each other. She completes me."

The tone in my mouth was forceful as it made the children quiet. Even Cedric stopped as I stated with shock, "You mean my friend Emma. The one that is married to your friend Henry?"

"Was married. She left him weeks ago and he has gone on with his life. They are getting a divorce and as soon as we can pay for it, we will get a divorce."

"Divorce?"

"Yes. You act like you didn't see the shit unfolding before your eyes. I don't fuck you for weeks at a time and when I tried it wouldn't get up because it doesn't want you."

"Don't want me?"

"No! Even if I didn't have her, I wouldn't want you."

I wanted to fall, but my children had me standing as he said, "Look, she makes me smile and I don't hear the bullshit from her I get from you. She smells good, she takes very good care of me in every aspect, and she is never like you, a nagging ass disappointment."

2

With tears in my eyes and a knife in my heart I mellowed out the words, "Forget about how you feel about me. What about your babies? Our babies?"

He looked at the girls and gave them each a kiss on the forehead to say, "Angela, you're always taking care of them. You can do it, but you won't do it with me. Besides, what is the difference now? They already get your time, anyway. Think of this as a get out of jail free card."

"Get out of jail free card?"

Cedric sounded almost joyful as he exclaimed, "Yes. You are no longer bound to deal with me and me with you. We only have the girls in common, and you can have the responsibility all by yourself. I don't have a police job yet, but she has a lot of income. For now, no child support from me, but when I get on my feet I will help."

"You are my husband. How are you just gone leave us high and dry?"

Cedric yelled at me to the top of his lungs, "Angela I don't want to be your husband anymore. Are you not listening? Can't you see? Why do you think I am leaving your dumb ass?"

Silently but in a confused state I bellowed out, "I don't know why? You come in complaining and not trying to talk to me. You must communicate with me for me to understand what is happening to us."

He gave me a look like I stink as he took a garbage bag. He walked off and opened the cabinets to clean out the canned food, dry goods, like the meal, flour, sugar, beans, and rice. I just stood there and watched as he moved in record speed. Cedric walked towards the fridge. I went right behind him as he snatched another garbage bag from the top and loaded it up on the meat. He picked up the pint of milk and put it in there, it was already opened. Lyn asked, "Why taking food, daddy?"

I said with sarcasm and pain, "Yeah, daddy why take the food out of our mouths?"

With a smile and a touch of her cheek, he leaned to Lyn, and spoke with joy, "Momma gonna buy you some more. She gonna buy you what you like."

"Okay," Lyn said as she held onto me with a smile.

Little Rossi cried and tugged on my hair. I could barely pay attention to her as I uttered out loud to him, "You know I don't have a job or a way to pay the extra bills or buy food. I don't get stamps until the end of the month. Remember you said we were behind on utilities and rent last month as you sold all the stamps."

As if he thought of something to say, he spoke as if he didn't know what to think, "You have a money maker, shake it."

My mouth dropped as he said that. He shrugged, got another garbage bag, and went to the bathroom. I walked quickly as I could behind him to see what he was going in there for. He started packing all the soap, toothpaste, deodorant, bath towels, and tissue. Lyn asked, "Why taking tissue and sup, daddy?"

I sounded like a child, as I said, "Daddy, you are taking the tissue and sup, too?"

Cedric glanced up me, but said to Lyn, "This is old. You will get some newer tissue and soap."

"Okay," Lyn said as she saw her dad stripping us of closed bare necessities.

He left the bathroom and walked outside to put the garbage bags in the truck. He came back and grabbed his suitcase and walked back outside. With my children still attached to me, I walked like Frankenstein outside behind him as fast as I could. He put the suitcase in and jumped in his brand-new black F-150 extended cab truck. I yelled with tears and little strength, "What am I going to do? I don't have anything. You have taken everything!"

From his moving truck he hollered out, "You'll figure it out. You always do."

Right then and there I became lost as the sight of his truck went out of sight. I placed my hand on my heart and dared it to feel. I needed to make sure it was still working because he just broke it, stomped it, and smashed it to pieces. The girls began to whine louder because they were hungry and so was I. My husband took all the money we had without making groceries. We went into the house, and I locked the door. I put the girls to the table to see what he left us. I opened the fridge and only saw butter and a half a loaf of bread. *At least he didn't take that,* I thought as I saw my two babies crying.

Rossi pulled on my hair, and I glanced at her with a smile as she said, "Hungry."

"Okay," I spoke with joy.

I fixed them butter toast. I didn't eat. I couldn't eat. My oldest asked, "Momma, you not eat?"

"Baby, momma's not hungry" I spoke gently.

"Daddy coming back?" Lyn asked.

"I don't know, baby. Finish eating so you can get plenty of rest and grow big and strong."

"Strong like daddy?"

It bothered me to hear the word daddy, but I bit my tongue and said with ease, "Just like daddy."

My daughter started back eating her toast as I fed Rossi hers in small portions. I have a mountain of bills and a bleeding heart, which I never thought I would have. Everything I ever had, included my family was sitting with me looking lost. I thought I was doing everything right. Then

I thought *when Rossi came along, we had no more quality time. He would always leave when he got off from work. I stayed home to cook, clean, and took care of the children and the house. I had no idea how bitter and hateful Cedric had become. He would complain and when asked about it, he would say it's nothing, so I let it go.*

I never assumed another woman was in the picture, especially Emma. I knew I could be replaced, but to be replaced because of life situations was another thing. I used to work as a Paralegal until the driver of an eighteen-wheeler fell asleep, ran the red light, and smashed into me. I had bad back problems, and it was hard for me sometimes. The good thing was I got one hundred thousand dollars as back pay. When the lawyer finished, I only ended up with a little over fifty thousand dollars, and disability with a fixed income of seven hundred and fifty dollars a month.

Cedric controlled the money, which was fine with me. We paid down the house, bought furniture, and he bought the family the brand-new truck, which I could never drive or ride in because the children always made a mess. Plus, he was always gone to work in it and when it came to doctor appointments, I had to call the Medicaid people for a ride. My cousin, Tammy, thought I was stupid in love and took far too much, but I kept assuring myself it was all for the love of my family.

7

However, he didn't start acting so odd until after we started going to church. Once I became baptized in the Holy Ghost he changed on me. On the weekends, he went riding with his friends while I stayed home. I was getting tired of watching the show of my life being played out before me and not actually being able to participate in it. I told Cedric of my feelings. He said he would watch the children while I went out with Tammy. All the time when it came time for me to leave, he always had something to come up. I got used to being put on the back burner for him and him not pulling his fair weight. It made our living conditions worse.

The only good thing to come out of this was the babies. I sniffled and Lyn began to cry. I stared down in her green eyes and smiled. I know I must be strong for them and being strong is the only thing not taken from me today. Just never thought I would be a single parent this early in the game. I focused back to my children and saw how ironic it was the most Lyn ever talked about her dad. I didn't know if it was a reminder for me or the devil used my daughter to pull me down further than I already felt.

When they finished, I took them a bath and put them down to rest. For a long time, I watched all I had sleeping in their twin bed. I heard of women being a single parent and doing it all by themselves, but I never pictured me doing it. I thought of Tammy. *She had a child named Andre. I watched*

how she struggled to raise him, but she did. Andre was
fifteen and he never lacked anything. I would always tell her
I plan to wait until I get married to have children.

I decided to have a seat to think, I went to the rocker
and began rocking. I didn't want to bathe as I sat in the chair
staring at the highway Cedric took. I sighed, as I felt all
emotional and angry at the same time. I shook my head to
shake my thoughts and the day's event, but it did no good. I
reached up to my face and tears trickled some. I opened my
mouth to cry, but a sound would not come out of a dry
mouth. I rocked a few times as realization finally hit me. I
was about to embark on the journey of my lifetime.

Making a sound of hopelessness I went on and took a
long bath. I went to bed and closed my eyes. The next
morning and the mornings after that were hard. I would wake
up crying and go to bed crying. I did my best not to let the
girls see me, but I couldn't help it. I would tell them my back
ached or something of that manner. For the most part I tried
keeping them busy by watching cartoons or coloring to keep
their mind off their father. It worked in the day for them, but
at night, Lyn would bawl for him and so did I.

The next twenty-one days were rough, then the first
came and so did Cedric. He wanted to prove to me that he
made a mistake and wants his family back. I still love him,
and I know he loves me despite the things he said to me. The

girls wanted their daddy, and I needed my husband. Going against how I really felt, I decided to give it a chance. I had to make sure I have done all I could to keep the family together even if it meant taking his lying cheating ass back.

The next few weeks rolled in, and Cedric would come by. We started back seeing each other like he wanted but living in different houses. He told me that he and Emma are not together and how he is living with a friend on the police force. My heart told me not to do it, but my body wanted to have my husband and even if we aren't living as we should. I believe that all will work out to my advantage. He would come over and I would have dinner done as we all would sit at the table like a real family, nothing out the ordinary. At night when we put the girls to bed, he would put me to bed by making mad passionate love to me.

There were times I didn't want him to touch me because he has had her, but my body wanted him just as much as he wanted me. I told myself I had forgiven him and that means total forgiveness for the stress he placed upon the girls and me. I did think about how he could do this to me again or what I would do if he broke my heart all over again. I didn't want to think of the "what if" possibilities because I refused to borrow trouble. He was being the man he needed to be in the beginning, and I was letting him.

For starters, he did things for me he hadn't done in years. He even let me drive the truck to run errands while he was at work. The girls were happy to see him come home and so was I. Cedric had me rethinking his actions from every angle. Maybe I should keep it like that until we can live in the house again, but I wanted to see my husband all the time and not on his days off and in between. It hadn't been like that in a long time, and I believed all was well just like he said.

We lived the married life without the hustle and bustle of being under one roof. I put it in my head that I was still a married woman but had single intentions with my husband. Cedric would call me beautiful at my worst and compliment me at my best. My husband knew when to butter me up and how to do it. When I felt down, he would lift me up and make me smile like only he could do. He was joyful and not stressed about life and so was I. Maybe us like this is what is best, but I knew it wasn't; although, I was happier than I had been in a long time.

It was the simple fact that my husband and I would take the girls to the park and even did house chores together. We would horse play in the house, and he would play tea games with the girls. Cedric allowed them to put makeup on him and comb his long hair. He showed me how he had changed in such a few weeks of separation. When the first and third came, I would give him the money as usual, and he would pay the bills and do what he may need to do. It all was working out for the better. I was anxious to see him and anticipated every chance to be with him when he would come over.

Like usual we put the girls to bed and made love throughout the night. I had a thought of having a son would be the cure for our dysfunctional marriage, but I don't need to bring another child into the mess we already have now. However, after a wild night of fucking, he went to sleep and for some reason, I couldn't. My mind was in one hundred directions, and none led to Cedric. It was a weird feeling of all good things must come to an end. I was uneasy about it and tried to play it off.

It was one in the morning, and I got out of bed to watch him sleep. His cell phone was on silent, but it lit up. It caught my attention. I walked over to the night table and put the phone in my hand. I went to the living room and from the moment I flipped open the phone my short-lived happiness came to a stop. I saw a naked pic of Emma with a message that read: dream of this when you hitting that, lol.

I began to speed-read every text on his phone and all the texts that he and Emma did. I felt like shit with flies flying all around it. He has played me again and this time it hurt worse than the first. I knew I shouldn't have taken him back so soon, but I needed to be with my husband. I needed to be loved and to be with the man I loved, but that was a lie. From what I gathered, Emma was trying to do to Henry what Cedric was doing to me, except Henry didn't buy it like I did.

The text read like a game plan for them to get their old lives back, but still trick off. He told her how he missed fucking her and how she can only please him. He said he missed the multiple ways they would make out, among others. They were conversing as if my heart and love were a game. They had no thought to what all this was doing to my daughters, who assumed their parents were reconciling. How about me or the persona I had of us?

Sobbing and blowing snot everywhere was an understatement. I cried like a frog, calling out for water during a drought. The pain was so unreal and thought of as a bad dream, but I know better. He intentionally toyed with my heart for the second time. Cedric made me cry harder than anyone has ever had in my life. The way I felt about the man I called a husband is a feeling I would not wish on my worst enemy.

I went back to my bedroom and began hitting him. He woke up, trying to defend himself. I was crying harder now than I did a few minutes before. Cedric finally got out the bed, and yelled, "What the fuck yo ass doing! I was fucking sleep!"

"Emma sent you a naked pic," I said as he displayed a *how can I explain this shit* look on his face. I stated with tears. "You still fucking seeing her! How could you do this to me and the girls all over again!"

"She just mad," he called out.

"No, the fuck she ain't. I read every text in your phone to and from her. You played me. You fucking played me you piece of shit. You had me to believe we were getting back together, but I tell you this, you won't see this again. Now get the fuck out of here before I call the police and have you escorted out of here and if I never see you again, I won't cry about it!"

He got his things and didn't say a word as I threw his phone at him. For an hour or two I couldn't sleep. I tried, but the images of the text haunted me like sin to a Christian who knew better. For the next few days, nothing I tried worked. Sleep would not come to me. When my body crashed and I did fall asleep, I awoke to the smell of smoke. Coughing and choking, I got up quickly and went for my children. Snatching them out of their sleep, I went as fast as I could to the outside. I didn't even close the door because I heard a boom sound as we fell to the ground.

14

The house went up in flames. Neighbors came to our rescue as they took the girls and helped me off the ground. I just stood there in disbelief and surprised because the fire department was too late to save my house. The girls cried as I cried. *This cannot be happening to me;* I thought as I stood there overwhelmed as my new friend. First my husband is caught in his web of lies, and then the house suddenly catches fire. The Fire Marshall came over to consult us. He asked, "Do you have family you can stay with?"

I turned and looked at him to say, "Not really. It's complicated."

"I see. We can put you all up for the night. Will it be fine?"

"Yes, please."

"Ok it'll be a few minutes" he said as he walked off.

The girls were still half asleep, but I was fully awake and homeless. The kindness of the man made me feel better. When we arrived at the hotel, the clerk showed us to our room and left. I put the girls in their bed as I sat there. A knock was heard, and it was the clerk. She said, "My dad is the Fire Marshall, and he told me you all lost everything."

"We did."

"I know this is not much, but it will help."

The young girl gave us some clothes. Their generosity made my voice crack and tears fell. She gave me a hug and I could feel the tears. She didn't know all the things that had happened in a short length of time, but a genuine hug was needed. I cried for what seemed like hours. I realized this girl was at work and there I was, stopping her from doing her job because my husband has rejected us to do him. She looked at me with compassion to say, "Here is fifty dollars."

"I can't take it. I know you need it."

"Ma'am please take this from me. Let me be a blessing, so in return I can get blessed."

"No one has ever done anything like this for me."

"Well, there are still good people out there; although, many have made it hard for those who are truly in need to get the benefits they need. I am glad to be some help to you and your precious ones."

"You have shown me more thoughtfulness than their father has. I am eternally grateful for this in my time of need."

"I don't mind. My parents brought me and my brothers up knowing if you can help someone help them. If you can't, point them in the best direction as possible."

"I hope I can instill those values in my girls" I added.

"You will. I don't know your situation, but I believe God for you."

"Thank you."

I took the money and gave her a hug. She released me to say, "All I ask is you pay it forward."

"I will to whoever, when I get on my feet."

"Okay. I must go. Have a good night. Well, what's left of it."

I smiled as she continued, "If you need me, call the front desk."

When she left, I sat on the bed. It crossed my mind how my husband never called to check on us. I thought *this bastard really does not care about me or our kids.* For the first time in a long time, I lay down and prayed: **"Lord, I don't know what to do. I have two children depending on me and I don't have a job. Lord, I know the little money I receive may not be enough for us to live on. I ask you to bless it and guide me on what to do. I can't let this break me. You can do exceedingly and above all great things, for that I am grateful. Please wrap your arms around me and strengthen me. Amen."**

I lay on the bed, crying and didn't remember going to sleep. I just remembered praying out my soul. I opened my eyes and looked at my girls. They were still sleepy and at peace. I called Tammy. She was a Pharmacy Tech and does insurance on the side. When she answered, she asked, "Ange why you at a hotel?"

"My house burned last night."

"Your what?"

"My house burned last night."

"Everybody ok?"

"Yeah, but Cedric is not with me."

"What you mean, not with you?"

"We split up and were working things out, but not living together and I caught him lying and still being with the other woman."

"That bastard did what?"

"He went back to the woman he left me for. The bastard played me, Tammy. He fucking played me."

She was quiet before saying, "You and the girls can come stay with me and Andre."

"You know we can't. You have your own things going on. You don't need me and my issues."

"I don't care. You my girl and I won't leave you and yours out like that. You family and have you ever known me to not help you when you need it?"

"I never known you not too help me."

"Right, so how you talking?"

I did a gentle laugh as I replied, "I know your boyfriend is jealous and doesn't like us talking too much."

"Yeah, but he comes over when I tell him to."

"Well, I can stay until we get the insurance money."

"You did pay the insurance, didn't you?"

"Yes. Cedric paid it last week or the week before last when it was due. I'm not too sure, but I do know he paid it."

"Ok. Let me check for you right quick."

She put me on hold for a few minutes and said, "Let me call you back. I got to check something."

I hung up and the clerk knocked on the door to say, "Good morning."

"Good morning."

"You all sleep well?"

"Yes. The girls are still asleep."

"That's good. Check out is at noon. Here is a number to a homeless shelter and the Women Helping Women Outreach Center. They will give you food, clothes, furniture, and anything else you may need, if you need it."

"This means so much to me. Thank you so much. Tell ya dad I said thank you, too."

"I will. I came by to let you know some people at my church took up a donation and here it is."

She handed me an envelope. I gave her a hug and she left. I sat down and opened it. I cried. It was five hundred dollars in it. While the girls slept, I took a bath. When I came out the room, Lyn had the TV on. She saw me, and asked, "Our house got fire, mommy?"

"Yeah, it's gone."

"We get a new one?"

"I hope so."

"Where daddy?"

"He had to work. You know daddy always work and I'm sure he will see you and Rossi soon."

"Ok. I'm hungry."

"Wait until Rossi wakes up and we will go get some food."

She said, "Okay" as she turned back around and began watching cartoon again. I removed the towel and put on the clothes. I thank God, the clothes were a perfect fit. Rossi finally woke up and I wiped them both off. Before we could leave the phone rang. I slowly said "Hello."

"Ange, you're sitting down?"

"No. Do I need to?"

"I think you need to."

"What is it?"

"That bastard husband of yours did not pay the insurance. In fact, your insurance has not been paid since you got the house. He even cashed out the life insurance, which totaled up to be about seven thousand dollars."

I slowly sat on the bed and dropped the phone. I knew he was paying it because I saw the receipts and knew the bills were all paid. Lyn asked, "Mommy you dropped the phone," as she handed it back to me.

Tammy said, "Ange you, ok?"

"Tammy, how can I be all right? I saw the receipts of the insurance. Are you sure? Did you make a mistake?" I said with my heart in my ears.

"Girl, this is about money. You know I did not make a mistake. It's my job to keep up with what has been paid. In fact, I will print it out for you."

"I have nothing," I spoke, dryly.

"You and the girls made it out alive and that is what matters."

"It is what matters."

She was quiet as, she asked, "Has the piece of a husband of yours called you to check on y'all?"

"No."

"What the fuck! I mean what?"

"I haven't heard from him since I caught him lying."

"The bastard didn't leave y'all with shit."

"Nothing."

"Y'all can still come and stay with us."

"Make sure it is ok with James."

"I got this. You just be there at the hotel when I get there by twelve."

The line was quiet as, I said, "This is so much for me to digest."

"Girl, eat that shit and keep it moving. Stuff like this happens a dime a dozen. I must help bring you up to date on some things."

"Like what?"

"I'm going to save the sermon for this evening," Tammy said as she laughed.

"Yeah, I know it is coming."

"It is, but don't worry about it. It's the little things like getting you a cell phone, dating sites, and a Facebook Page."

"I am still married. Leave out the dating sites."

Tammy could hear my expression in my tone and changed her excitement. This time she softens her voice, "Ange you are married to a man who has showed you on more than one occasion how he doesn't want to be married to you. So, cut the dumb shit and get with it. Fuck him. When he left y'all he clearly said fuck you. Even if he didn't say it with his mouth his actions told you." I was quiet as she said, "Ok I am taking you too fast, but when I finish with you, his ass gon' wish he had you back."

"Tammy, it just came to me he really doesn't care about me, but the children. He really doesn't want us."

"Ange welcome to the world of single mothers."

CHAPTER 2

Tammy came and picked us up. The girls were happy to see her because she buys them things I won't. She gave me a hug as I strapped the girls down. I got in and Tammy smiled at me. I know she is excited about having us at her home because we use to visit a lot before my accident a year before. I glanced over my shoulder and saw my girls were looking out the window and enjoying the ride to Tammy's house.

When we arrived at her beautiful home, we each unlocked a child. Tammy said that Andre was gone for Spring break and will return on Sunday. James was gone and won't be back for another two weeks. I was glad because I don't want to cause any problems in her relationship because my husband has decided a family isn't what he wants. I sighed and she saw it. Giving me nice pat on the shoulder, I gave her a smile and followed her.

She was leading us to the guest room upstairs. I have always liked her home, but it was too extravagant for my taste, but it's still a lovely place. Tammy took the bikes by the hand and said, "I took the rest of the day off, so when you finish doing what you doing come outside. We can watch the children play as we talk."

"Ok."

She walked off with the girls and sat in the bed before going outside. When I reached the yard, Lyn and Rossi were playing in the small sand pit, Tammy had put in a year ago just for the girls. We sat under the umbrella on the patio set as Tammy had her drink and handed me a Coke. She said, "Ok. I want to tell you I am sorry about you losing all you had. I know starting over is not easy, but you have it made better than I did."

"Thank you. I'm still dazed about it all, but how I have it better than you did?"

"I have money to help you. When I was out on my luck, you put me and my son up. You went all out your way to make me happy. I didn't forget how it meant a lot to me."

"I remember, but I didn't do it for you to return the favor. I did it because I love you and your family."

"I know you didn't, but I have a little change that I call tittie money put up and tucked away."

"Tittie money?"

"Every woman has her own rainy-day money stashed away for times such as this."

"I don't."

"That is because he always controlled all the money you had, but now it is time to be in control of your own shit, girl. Don't let another man know everything about you or how you get what you get and importantly where you get it from."

"I agree. I just don't know how? This is so new to me."

"Stick with me and you will, trust me."

"You know I trust you."

She took a sip of her drink and said, "We going to give you a makeover."

She put her drink down, got up and looked at my hair. She picked it up and said, "You have too many split ends. When is the last time you got it professionally fixed?"

"It has been so long, I can't remember, but I think it was a year before Rossi was born."

"That's too long. Too damn long" Tammy spoke as she giggled.

"I been busy, and time just went by."

"You let yourself go. You didn't do it on purpose it just happened, but I am going to make it un-happen." I laughed at her as she said, "I'm serious. You are beautiful and he knows it. He just took it for granted and now he has lost it."

"You think?"

"I do, but I know it is going to take some work because you are simple, which is fine, but nowadays put on some thongs, half dressed, let him see what he is missing in you. Even let your feet hang out."

"If it were that easy, I would have done it a long time ago," I spoke with a little laughter.
"I don't mean to curse, but hell you in my house and this is the way I talk. I don't mean any harm and I don't want to offend you, but shit, fuck that fucking shit. Bitch, do you like never before."

"I understand ya" I said with laughter.

"Now that is out the way. As I was saying, sometimes it takes losing to win."

It made kind of made sense as I questioned my best friend, "Losing to win?"

"Don't get it, just understand it."

This time I did laugh loudly as I stated, "I can't get what I don't understand."

She sat back down and said, "A war has many battles and during those battles you win, and they may win, but it's who comes out on top in the end is what matters. That alone determines the winner. Cedric won a battle by leaving you high and dry with shit, but kids and bills. Now you win and you win again." She put her drink down and began pounding her fist into her hand, when she said, "You keep hitting and striking that mother fucker until he falls." She picked up her drink again, and said, "It's not revenge or karma, but shit, let

26

the fucker see what he doesn't have anymore. Quit responding to the pity party invitation and say goodbye to the old you and announce your true self." I kept shaking my head to agree with her because she was correct on everything she said. Tammy saw me shaking my head to agree with my mind. I glanced over, and she sounded softer, "Be head strong. You can do it. I know you can, Ange. You just need to feel you can. You have potential to get it together quick. When I was a single parent, I had only one depending on me. You have two little people depending on you, counting on you to come on with it. Girl, it's going to be now or never, but I see your problem."

"What is my problem?"

"You made his hustle your only hustle. Once you start bringing your own steaks, he'll wonder where you get your food from. Trust me I know what I am talking about. There have been many times, I had to do for me and mine. I'm not proud of all my decisions, but it is what it is. Trust and believe I know what I am talking about."

"You sound like you do."

"I do. Shit you looking at a bitch that had to learn the hard way. The difference is I had no choice and you had Cedric; therefore, that made you not having to do like me."

"Looks like, I should have been listening and watching."

"True, but now is what matters. I went through that spell to help you."

I looked over at my girls and saw how happy they were. They are untainted from all this, and I am glad they don't know as they would if they were older. Tammy said a lot of good things, but I was nervous. This whole new world was frightening to me. Tammy noticed my uneasiness as she said, "I know this is not easy for you, but hell if it were easy a lot of us would do it but it's not. I know you spent your life being the good girl and being raised by Grandma didn't make you hard. The way Grandpa played her ass, shit she should have been in a bitch class to take notes herself."

That was funny as I reached over and tap her hand. Tammy added, "I'm for real. He was doing him while she was being the wonderful wife and what did that get her? It got her a stepchild with two heartaches."

"Yeah, it did, didn't it. That betrayal hurt her so much she died of a broken heart."

"I think so, but I'm serious. Her ass should have been asking those bitches what the fuck she needs to do to keep his old, tired ass at her house."

"You so hard" I stated with a smile.

"It's not that I'm hard, but you have to be hard if you expect to make it on your own. No one is going to just give you shit, but a hard time and a mediocre dick. They might have if you are married, but that doesn't work."

"Why cheat if you are in a sacred relationship or with someone you claim to love?"

She laughed a loud laugh and sat up to speak directly to me, "For me it was just to see how it was to be the other woman. I know what I went through when I was the main woman. I will never forget the countless nights I cried these eyes red and puffy or the days when I wouldn't eat. One day I woke the fuck up and decided that crying was not a part of my DNA anymore. Ever since I made that pact with my eyes, these bitches only cry tears of joy."

"Seriously?" I asked with a smile.

"Yes. I wanted to be the woman on the outside to see just how Andre's dad did it to me. I couldn't see it from my point of view, so I changed sides. When I started doing it, I was scared at first, no lie. But as time went, I saw just how easy it was for him to do it to me, and it was extremely easy. The lies he told me I perfected them back to him and he ate it, just like I used to. I have done it so long, that I like the variety of dick I can get when I want and how I want."

"You're saying it's easy to cheat, go home to the one you love, and sleep by them at night, with no remorse?"

"I mean, when you get back home to the home dick, you don't want him to put his arms around you or nothing because he could ruin your excitement. I can lie and lay beside my man and sleep like a baby, unless you lie about being somewhere like going on a plane and it crashed, and then you have to think on your feet. The kicker is you tell your conscious to shut the hell up and let you do you and after a while it listens. Problem solved."

"Maybe it kept talking and you didn't listen."

"That is more than likely what happened," she said with a smile as she tasted her drink.

"You know who he is seeing now don't you?"

"Already? His ass just left."

"I know."

"Who is the bitch to do you a favor? Tell me so we can shake her damn hand together."

I smiled, and said, "Emma."

"Young ass twenty something year old Emma that married to Henry what's his face?"

"Darling."

"Yeah, that's it. I used to fuck with his lame ass cousin. Shit he hooked me up on the game I run now," she exclaimed as she jumped up from her chair.

"Well, he told me she is his everything and even if he didn't have her, he wouldn't want me."

Her mouth dropped opened. It hurt even more to even repeat it. I spoke on, "I loved him, flaws, and all. He isn't perfect and not even in the top five, but love is love. I just assumed he felt the same way or at least we started off that way. Somehow or another I became married to myself and the girls."

Tammy said as she slurps down her drink, "You see shit like that pisses me off. I can understand if you were like me, but you aren't. You a good girl and he just hung himself. Now more than ever I am more determined to make him pay for it all."

We giggled at that as she said, "Why were you trying to make your yard dog a house pet, anyway?"

"My yard dog a house pet?" I questioned back to her.

"Any time your dog runs around in the yard, he's going to eventually get in the road and chase everything in it. You see my dog is a jealous dog. He sees me in the road, and he barks. I know he's going to want to know what I am doing in the road and the day he does, it is the day I get a new dog. I don't have time to run behind dick. I'm too old of a cat for that."

We were quiet for a moment as she asked, "You are marriage material, and I applaud your type of women. I have been on my own too long and I don't plan to be caught up again in the shit you call love. That word alone will fuck your head up and get somebody hurt. After Andre's dad broke that muscle in my chest, which pumps blood to my

31

body. I vowed not to ever let another man do to me what he did. So, far I have been right."

I sighed, and replied, "I guess everyone is not ready for marriage as I thought Cedric was."

"He was ready for marriage just not ready for the responsibility that flowed with it. He thought being in a relationship would be peaches and cream until he saw responsibility."

"How is that when he had Lyn before he met me?"

"Everybody had Lyn not him. But, when he got you, he got Lyn back, and then Rossi then responsibility. You get the picture?"

"Yeah. I mean I thought we were happy and in love, Tammy."

"You were happy and in love, but I don't think he was. Life came and hit his ass, face first."

"Life and Emma's big butt," I added with a tease.

We snickered as she said, "You always gave all of you in all the relationships I have known you to be in. Stop placing all your money on the first hand. Play it awhile before you become completely broke. You never save anything for you. Ange, you never give it all away because you never know when you need some for yourself."

"Some like what?"

Tammy looked up as if she were thinking what to say, "Time, love, happiness, joy, feelings, emotions, and anything else you can think of that you don't have for yourself. I have seen you go without for him. You made sure he had what he needed, while, you had nothing. The main thing I didn't like was how you would tell him everything."

"I don't tell him everything."

"Yes, you did. You tell him everything. Let his sneaky ass wonder sometime how you got this and that. Let him try and figure you out. Don't be so damn readable all the time."

"I don't do secrets."

"I know you didn't, but you going to. I'm not saying cheat. That's for me. I'm just saying live. He's living. I can bet you any type of money that he is doing him."

"What you keep meaning by that?"

"I'm just saying if he wants to fuck, he gon' fuck. If he wants to eat steak and can't afford it somebody is going to buy it. He ain't settling, but you are. You take whatever part of him he gives you and you are content because you love him just that much. You see past all his shortcomings, and you never mention them to him, but he is so quick to throw up in your face all you are and are not doing. He knows he has you, but put something on his mind. Let him know you aren't afraid of being out of his shadow anymore. You can

33

still be classy and a mother at the same time. You don't have to be complacent for what you see. Put legs on your dreams and make them a vision to come to pass. Right now, he thinks you are going to pout around and wait on him while he does what he wants then come back to you. He is wrong. You are not going to do it because I won't let you. He has a friend. Get you a friend or two or three. Hell, if you can handle it juggle," Tammy laughed at that.

"You make it sound so easy, but it's hard for me to go from married to single."

"Let me school you on a few things and you will see just how easy it'll become."

I sat back, and said, "Tammy I actually thought he was ready for all of this."

Tammy put her drink down, and opened her arms wide to say, "Shit I ain't ready for all this and I have a fifteen-year-old. How the hell you talking?"

I laughed and spoke as Tammy started back drinking, "I did. I really thought he was ready. He was business headed, had his priorities straight, we dated a little while before we got married, and then Rossi came along, plus, he was loyal."

She threw her hand up as to stop me to say, "Now the last word you said right there doesn't mean shit to a cheating man or woman. You are only loyal to God. The rest of this is

34

flesh and will fuck your life up. It'll fuck you up so bad you wouldn't know if you were going or coming with your eyes open looking at the direction."

"I am beginning to see it now," I said with laughter.

"I'm for real. Loyal, faithful, honesty, commitment, trust, one lover, and some more fucked up words don't mean shit do you hear me? They don't mean shit in a dog ass world like the one we live in. Back in the day those were the words like the bible. You lived by those words, and those words went a long way. In this time, those words leave your mouth and fall to the damn ground right there," she said as she pointed from her mouth to the ground.

I laughed, and said, "Well call me crazy, but I based my love and my marriage on that. I never thought I would be living my life without my husband; nevertheless, married but single."

"Don't get me wrong, Ange. Those words are good basis if the man is being on the real with you. Let me say it like this, if a man is being all those words to you then hell yeah give some of them back to him. Don't ever give a dog your all. I wouldn't trust that bastard if he told me he was down the road, on side of the road, out of gas, on a flat, with one headlight and one taillight and he couldn't come home because he couldn't see, and its day light."

It was too funny. Tammy said, "You need to change breeds better yet change dogs. You have had this mutt too long and your top-notch breed, Ange. We going to make him wish he had kept you because you are rare, a jewel. All he had to do was take you off the shelf, polish you up, and then put you back up. But no, he wants to throw you back in the deck for another man to pick you out and play with you for a little. Are you listening?"

"I'm listening."

"No, you not. You are hardheaded and it's going in one ear and out the other."

"I am listening" I spoke earnestly.

She drunk some more and said, "I really do understand your pain, but get over it, Ange. You can't keep putting up with him and his ways. Either he wants you or he doesn't. He has showed you the door and not just you, but the little Lyn and Rossi, too. They don't deserve the way he has done them. They are worthy to be in a home with parents who will love them, and it doesn't have to be the DNA dad, either."

When we finished speaking, we looked over at the girls. They were playing quietly in the sand pit. They had fun and their joyful sounds touched my heart. I so much want them to be happy because I was happy when I was their age. I knew the importance a male father can have on your life, and I wanted and desired that much for them. There is so much I can teach them and so much a father can. I took my eyes off them to ask, "How do I do it?"

"You get on your shit and stay on your shit. Let that fucker see you happy. He dealt a blow and it's cool. He's allowed a lick every now, and then, but now you know better and there are no more hits for him."

"I'm going to try it your way, but I still plan to keep going to church. I might have to find a new one."

"Who says you can't? There are more divorced church going women in church than there is in the club. You going to do you, but you are going to do you better."

"You so sure, Tammy?"

We were quiet for a minute. Tammy said, "I am so sure because I am going to help you all I can. His bastard ass not paying the insurance is fucked up."

"It was, wasn't it?"

"Girl, for the record your husband won't know a good thing if it stared him in the face; nevertheless, be married to it."

"I don't know how we went from sugar to crap overnight."

"You mean sugar to shit?"

I laughed, and said, "Well that."

"It didn't just happen overnight. It was always happening you were just into keeping up with the "do the right thing" you never saw it coming. I know he did, and he is a coward for not telling you. Hell, you might have wanted to play in the triangle. He should have been honest and let you decide for yourself instead of making up your mind for you. There are too many diseases out there to gamble with a life of another person."

"Didn't we grow up believing if you good you'll get good back to you?"

"We did, but we don't live in that era anymore. Time has changed a lot of things. The way we grew up believing and thinking was one of them. People are not into the good things now. They want underhanded things and being involved in another person's relationship. We have more divorces than anything now. It's the thing to have casual sex, to hit it and quit it or in some cases try to quit it. You want to be able to fuck anyone you want when you want with no regrets and no strings. Men do it all the time, women just now trying to catch up."

"Women can't."

"Wrong not all women can if she shut off how she feels. If she let her emotions in the party, the party is going to get crazy and crazy fast. Look, all the things you did for him is not going to be done by another woman. I don't think the woman he is with now is half the woman you are. The only thing she may have on you is, she has time for him, money, living above her means, which causes him to put out more. Trust me, he is celebrating now but wait until reality set in and he gets sick and needs his nasty ass washed. How about when he can't work, and she has to be the help meet like you are? She won't do it. Hell, the outside woman doesn't want to take your place they just want to share it from time to time. Being that I have been a side chick before, when a man tells me he has left home, I would send their "I'm leaving ass home" back home so fast their head will spin because I don't need all his time, just time to do me. Wait until they see the thrill is gone and the dust has cleared. Ange, you got it. You have it all to your advantage. Stand up and take it."

I stood up, and she said, "You do not look like you have had any child. You have a small pudge, but a nice thick shape and you are not ugly. You are incredibly beautiful and sexy."

We laughed as she said, "Let me show you the ropes so you can learn your own rope. When you get it, hang his ass with it."

I was quiet as I looked down at my wedding band. I remember the day I got it. I heard Tammy say, "Take the shit off your finger. You are not married anymore."

39

"I am technically still married legally, anyway."

"Just because you were married to him, didn't make him married to you. Now give it to me."

I went too slow as she got up and pulled it off my hand. I looked up at her like a lost dog. Tammy looked at the ring to say, "You will live, and you are going to get a real life and not the life, Cedric had placed you in."

"I have young girls."

"Look everybody cheats at one time or another."

"I don't believe in that. If I had, I wouldn't have gotten married."

"Not yet" she spoke over the rim of her glass.

"I don't think so," I spoke assuredly.

"When you start seeing him going on with his life, you are going to want a life, too, because you will deserve it. Believe me, your pussy will get hot and thumping. You gone want to go a humping."

I laughed at Tammy as she threw her butt in the chair. She always made me feel better about anything. I had to ask, "You cheat on James?"

"Hell, when I don't cheat on James."

"But James is so jealous."

"Because he knows I will get the fuck down when I want to. I love casual sex. That's the best dick you can get. You don't have to worry about keeping up with it or if you

40

see another dick, you can get it. I love it because no one gets mad if they know what you do from the door."

"Tammy, are you serious? I mean I never known you to cheat or do casual sex anymore."

"Because I know how to balance the two and before long so will you."

I stared at her as she said, "I see now it's going to take a lot of dog hours to train you."

"Dog hours to train me? You a dog trainer now?"

"Yes. You tried turning your yard dog into a house pet. It will not happen. It can't happen unless Jesus comes down here himself. Because HE knows many of us are not right. I have taken it upon myself to skillfully engage in the task of educating a dear family member on how to get results. Ange, you invested your short life in a marriage with a dog ass man and that's for real."

"I am ready to take class because as long as I keep doing the same thing, I will keep getting the same results. I must do something different."

"Now it is time for you to show him he didn't make you and the shit he pulled didn't break you, it made you stronger, independent, and alive as a woman."

CHAPTER 3

Over the next ten weeks, I went to bed at night, praying to Jesus for a peace of mind that HE says HE can give. I had a challenging time, accepting the pain and hurt of love as I cry myself to sleep softly. I did not want to wake the girls, and I did not want anyone to hear me cry, but the loneliness got to me. Sometimes, I would get up and sit by the window and see peacefully everything looked except inside of me.

At one point I almost called Cedric to tell him that he could have me and her as long as he was in my life, but I knew that was not the life I wanted. I just don't want to cry anymore, and the things Tammy spoke, were on point, but my heart was still in love regardless of how my husband felt. I could not turn off how I loved him. Then, it'll come back to my mind how much I really do love him. I wish I could forget it all, but it is not easy when you are in a situation that affects more than your future.

Parts of me wish I could stop like he did, but I couldn't. The more I would stare out the window the more I realized it isn't going to be easy, but it can be done. *Was it so hard to want a marriage to consist of a mother and father to raise their children? Was I that bad that he couldn't love me as he said he would? What did we do to make him want another woman over me and his children?* I thought about those questions because I came from a two-parent home and the common factor was all I ever wanted; although, they may not have shown their unhappiness, but there was nothing my grandparents wouldn't do for me.

I looked up at the sky, and said to the Lord, "Lord I know I have lived outside of YOU and YOUR direction. I haven't served YOU completely and just started going to church when I got married, but to be thrown to the dogs is new to me. I know YOU know all that happens in the lives of YOUR children, and I am no exception. Help me to distinguish the difference between giving up and being fed up. Amen."

I went to sleep, but this time when I opened my eyes, I had a different outlook about my life. The girls and I still haven't heard from Cedric, and I was sad about it, but I came to the point of knowing I must be on some new shit. When my foot hit the floor, I sat there not sure if I could stand, but with courage and determination I got up. I walked downstairs to the bathroom as Tammy called out, "You have a phone call." She walked over to me, and said, "Don't fall for it" as she handed me her cell phone. I knew it was my long-lost husband by what she said to me.

In a low tone, I stated, "Hello."

"Hi. You and the girls, ok?"

It was really Cedric. My ears straighten up just to hear the sound of his voice. I looked over at her and she shook her head no. I put my mouth back to the phone to say, "No we died weeks ago."

"You are still funny, Angela."

"And you are still missing, Cedric."

"Look I heard about the fire and knew you would be with Tammy."

"You should have heard about how you reneged on paying the fire insurance when you know good dog gone well, we had the money for it."

"You act like I knew the house was going to catch on fire before I placed the money back."

"That is the purpose of having insurance in case an accident happened, and one did."

"You with your cousin, Tammy, and she has money so you good."

"No, I'm more than good. I'm damn good. If you don't believe me. Believe the shit I'm about to do."

"I see you already picked up her attitude."

"If you aren't talking about the girls in fact don't talk about them. Leave us the hell alone like you did the day I caught you lying to me and the house burned."

I hung up and Tammy smiled at me. She gave me a hug, and said, "I am so proud of you. Married girl, where did the bitch attitude come from?"

"He says I have picked up your attitude."

"Well good. You about to learn some shit then. As for the bitch attitude, she was already in you. It just took his lazy ass to bring it out. Today, I want you to meet someone who can keep the girls."

"I don't know about letting a stranger keep my children."

"I know her. She used to keep Andre a lot. Mrs. Carlita Shepard runs a Child Care service in the neighborhood."

"Is it a mom-and-pop type?"

"No," she said as she laughed to continue. "It is legit. I am going to let you go by there and see it for yourself."

"How can I pay for it?"

"She can charge the government for it because you are homeless and in need of her service."

"In other words, I draw a check, and that helps."

"You know it. Now hurry up and get the girls dressed. She is waiting on us."

I went in the bathroom and came up just as quick. The girls were up, and I got them ready. Tammy was outside, waiting on us. We locked the girls down and

45

Tammy told the girls they will eat in a little bit, and they were fine with it. I must admit overall I have raised my girls thus far good. They are well-mannered and listen to adults, but they are still children. They know momma will do all she can for them, and I could not help but smile.

We made it to the childcare center. It was well lit and full of energy. The girls were jumping squirming to get up as they saw the place. Mrs. Shepard was in the office waiting on us. She is a nice person, and she showed me her credentials. I was extremely impressed with the rating and child to teacher ratio. The girls started today with her and will be there from eight to five. I liked that. I will have plenty of time to do what I need to do without worrying about the safety of my children.

We left the girls and Tammy decided that today was my make-over day as we drove a little way and parked. She was showing me the Square as she led me to the beauty parlor and nail shop. The outside screamed expensive and when we walked in and I said quickly, "I can't afford this place."

"You can't, but I can."

Tammy stopped in front of me to say, "Think of this as a blessing. Let me do this for you."

"You are the second person that has said that to me."

"Well listen to it."

46

"Ok."

The guy who is to work on my hair was a nice guy. I got my hair dyed, clipped, and style. When he finished, another man took me to his stall and did my nails and feet. It felt weird because I never had a manicure or a pedicure before and it will not be my last. The way I was being pampered was awesome. *So, this is what feeling pretty feels like when you can afford it,* I thought as I admired my own self. Honestly, I did not recognize me. I really looked amazing. I never knew what extensions and a higher self-esteem could do to a woman, but I am experiencing it.

Tammy squealed when she said, "See you look like a new person. I did not recognize you. I am still amazed at the transformation. Ange, you look too damn good. Now we must change your wardrobe."

"My dressing is bad."

"No, it's fine for a married woman, but you are no longer her or all of her at least."

I dropped my head and Tammy yelled at me, "Yo ass searching for quarters?"

"No. Why?" I spoke as I snatched my head up with surprise.

"You are a diva now. You do not drop your head for shit unless you are praying or picking up your daughters.

You have a lot to learn so yo ass needs to learn fast. Now let's get you some clothes. I already have the girls theirs."

"I appreciate all you are doing for me and the girls."

"Show me you really appreciate me. Make me proud by showing the bastard what he lost. Stand on your feet. I'm not saying it's going to be a cake walk, but you can do it. I got you."

I smiled. Tammy spoke with genuine heart, "Keep the smile because it will open doors for you."

We left out the salon and went shopping. I saw so many nice clothes. They were not of my fashion, but Tammy swears I need them to match the new me. She even went as far as to get rid of my socks because it is spring and not winter. I don't know how I am going to survive wearing no socks, but I'll be ok. I changed into the clothes, and I could not believe I looked like this. We got in the truck and left. Tammy says I wear baggy clothes, so I appear bigger than I really am. She was right. I put on a size smaller than what I normally get, and I do have a nice body, even the love handles weren't shabby.

I had always been ashamed of my body since the children came along, even, my self-confidence was an all-time record low. When I took pictures, I would hide in the back or make sure I was not seen. To me, I didn't want to be seen. I just wanted to live a life of being a mother and doing

48

all I could for my family. Cedric changed that. He made me unaware of how beautiful I really was. He would say you can be beautiful, but that was it. He never seemed interested in me or made me feel the love I needed him to feel for me.

I guess I wanted to do my job and make him proud of the woman he married then I thought, *what about the woman I was becoming? What about the woman that was dying and didn't know it? I had become hidden to who I was and to what I thought. I forgot that I still have a life. I forgot that you can't get lost time back. I know it was because I was so focused on Cedric and the children that I forgot about me, the real Angela. I really don't know how to be anything else, but a wife and a mother. Anything else was out my comfort zone.*

Family oriented and family values are the things I had always done and had. I did use to party with Tammy, but I was the wall flower or the shy one. While, she would dance, drink, and have casual sex at random. If she saw, you and you were talking good. She would see what you got. Sometimes, if my cousin wanted to get her freak on, she would get down in the daylight in the back of a truck for the excitement of being seen.

There have been instances she would have a threesome with a married couple, which, I was totally against. Sometimes, she would let a mere stranger record her and whoever having sex. Tammy has always been too wild and uncut for me. She liked sex parties and strip clubs, but not me. I was the cautious one. I understood non-promiscuous safe sex, relationship, love, and being monogamous. Jumping into something headfirst was never my key point. I must see whatever it is I was getting into before I even think about getting into it.

It's like the way I believed can no longer match with the way I must become. The truck made a stop at Wendy's. We got out and went in. Tammy got her a meal and I ordered one. She said, "I still can't get over how amazing you look. You are a freaking turn on, Girl!"

"I know me, too."

"Now we have to set you up a Facebook page and get you a cell phone. How do you go so long without one?"

"It is irrelevant to me because I never had one. I had to make a business call I would use Cedric's phone or set up the appointment by mail."

"I can't tell that lie. I go to sleep with mine in my hand and I keep it on my hip."

We began to eat. Tammy said, "Go get a refill on your drink."

"I don't need one."

"Girl go."

I got up and took my cup upfront. When I made my way back to the table, I saw Cedric. He was coming out the bathroom. I almost froze as he looked me in my face. He did a double take and questioned in an unfamiliar way, "Angela?"

"Yes Cedric?"

His eyes went all over me as I stood there all dressed up and smelling good. He asked again, "Angela that's really you?"

"Yes, I am Angela the mother of your children."

"You look WOW."

I walked off from him and went back to my seat. I could sense him still standing and staring. I asked, "Why you set me up?"

"I knew you wouldn't do it on your own, so I had to force your hand. Did you see the way he kept looking at you?"

"Yes, I did" I spoke with nerves.

"What did he say?"

"He just said my name twice and how I look wow. I said it's me the mother of your children and walked off."

"He still standing there looking at us, Angela."

"So."

"Be cool here he comes."

"Hey, Tammy," Cedric spoke, not looking at her but me.

"What do you want at our table? Ain't shit over here for you. Your family died in the fire."

"I already explained to Angela how I knew she was at your house."

"What the fuck that means if you didn't check on them? Those your kids and you haven't tried to call them or see them."

"I know they in good hands."

"Yeah, they aren't in your hands."

"Someone needs to shut you up Tammy."

"A man has to put something between both of my lips, if he wants to shut me up. I'm a greedy bitch and no one dick, or tongue gone satisfy me."

"You still Tammy, always talking about sex."

"Angela hurry-up and talk to this begging ass fool."

Cedric looked over at me, and said, "I'm sorry." He looked at her then back at me.

"Don't tell me. I ain't yo damn wife."

Cedric said, "You have a way with words, Tammy."

He faced my way to say, "Angela can I see you or can I pick you and the children up and take you to the park? I miss you. I miss you and the girls."

"Cedric the girl you miss died when you lied. There is no way you are going to resuscitate her."

"Well can I at least talk to you first?"

"I'll hear what you have to say."

"Ok. I will come over tonight by eight."

"That will be fine."

He faced Tammy's way to spit out, "Bye guard dog, Tammy."

"By begging ass Cedric."

He left as Emma was coming in. They got their food and left. Tammy said, "You know you done put something on his mind to see you like this."

"You think?"

"Didn't you see the way he was gawking at you?"

"I tried not to look at him."

"Oh. Well, he was all in your drink."

"You think so?"

"Ange it's like this. He wants to know what or who has made you transformed into the new woman. He is gonna want some of your ass for old time's sake."

"I don't think so."

"He's gonna throw that hook at you. I'm just asking you not to bite."

"He can want all he wants."

I laughed as she ate, and said, "He is coming over tonight because he wants some pussy. Can't you read between the lines?"

"Pussy from who?"

"If you can say who, you know from who."

"Well, he better get it from Emma."

"I feel like you gone mess up and give it to him but try to hold out. You don't need to fall so fast. He's still with her. He's not even trying to get his family back. He thinks he is going to string you along and still fuck off with a younger bitch. I've been there before, and I know what I am talking about."

I didn't say anything because I know I am a sucker for him I just don't want to be anymore. I don't want him to keep doing me like this and not be the man I need him to be for me and the girls. If he is like Tammy says he is, we may have a chance. Tammy touched my hand to say, "You, ok?"

"Yeah" I spoke softly because I never imagined seeing them together. He never took me out anywhere and if he did, we had to order from the ride and not eat in. Tammy stammered, "Ange, I know it must have been hard to see them together in public."

"It was and I want to cry right now."

"I know you do, but you won't. The crying spells will get better, and time will heal all wounds if you let it."

"You're right. I have to see him and my life for what it is. I can't continue to be in this fantasy world, which only exists in the movies and not in my world."

"It's going to be ok. Keep listening to me and you will see how what you need to see."

I gave her a mock smile, and she said, "Eat so we can go. We have a lot to plan for tonight and I know being alone with him is one of the biggest test you are going to face this early in the game. Although, it is a big test because you haven't had any other dates yet."

"Don't you think it's too soon?"

"Ange this is the new age. Hell, his ass didn't waste time so, why should you? Get out your way of thinking for once. If you meet a guy you want to fuck; do it."

I laughed as she said, "Personally if a man don't lick; he don't stick shit over here."

I laughed some more at her as she asked, "What? Cedric don't eat pussy?"

I didn't say a word as she said, "I bet you have sucked his cheating dick."

"We have not done that since Rossi, and I don't care to do it now. There's no telling where he's putting it these days."

"You right. We need to get your pussy ate. I bet you he eating Emma's young tender pussy."

"Shush you talking too loud," I said as I looked around to see who all heard it.

"Come on. Leave this shit here. We got to get your freak on before you are left alone with Cedric, so you won't fall for his bullshit ass lies and fuck the bastard."

We left out of Wendy's, and I got a cell phone. Tammy taught me how to work it and I learned quickly. She was astounded that I picked up so soon. I had to admit I used to play around with Cedric's that's why I wanted one like his. We left there and made our way to the Naughty and Sweet Tooth Shop on the other side of town. I was reluctant to walk in, but went in.

The place had the atmosphere of sex all in it. I saw all kinds of sex toys and body oils. I even saw lingerie and other things I didn't know about. Tammy said here. I held my hand out and she placed a huge cock in my hand. I almost dropped it because she caught me off guard. She laughed at me as I asked with giggles, "Why you do that for?"

"You needed to feel a real dick in your hands before you see the dick you married."

She and I giggled when I said, "A dick in my hands?"

"It's better than the one you were with."

I could only shake my head as we walked around the store and pick up a few items. Tammy said she is going to see James this weekend and she has surprises for him. We went back to her house as she went in her room. I took the toy she bought for me and was nervous. I began to pep talk myself, "You can do it Ange. It's just a dick not hooked to a lying cheating man like Cedric."

Laying back I opened my legs and laughed because it was different. I pleased myself and was speechless at how real it was. Tammy was right. If I hadn't done this I would have caved like a hole in the ground for Cedric, but now he won't be getting this. Changing clothes, Tammy knocked on the door, and I yelled out, "Come in."

She looked around and asked with a smile, "Well did you get the edge off, or you need some help?"

"I did it myself, thank you."

"Well," she said as if it was Christmas morning, and she was getting the toy of her dreams.

"It was ok."

"Told ya, but we have to find you a man who will eat pussy."

"Here we go again with oral sex."

"I know at our age we want stability and the good stuff but until all that comes, we have to get with the program or get rebooted. You are twenty-seven and I'm thirty-one so trust your older cousin."

"Fine" I stated as I laughed.

"We have about another two hours before we pick the girls up from Mrs. Shepard. Until then we are going to start up you a few pages."

For over an hour, we set up dating pages, and a Facebook page. We added mostly men we did not know. Tammy posted my picture. I had never had so many notifications to come to my phone. I liked the single lifestyle. I didn't have to answer to Cedric about anything. It was like freedom I hadn't experienced before. I know why he doesn't want responsibility. It is a more convenient and less stress.

I felt like I could really do as my cousin said. I knew it would take some time, but I was willing to do what I must. There is no turning back for me and I don't like not knowing what the unknown is like. I like to know what my next step is, but when this happened, I was without a plan and without money. My children became fatherless, homeless, and starving all because of life choices. It pains me to hear them crying and I couldn't do anything about it. There was a time when they never cried unless they were being chastised.

It was not their fault if their dad was a cheapskate. They didn't ask to be born or brought into this loveless marriage. That bastard Cedric would pay. I don't care if I have to let him think I am fucking all his friends just to get him pissed. It was not that I want them, but the principle of it is he ran off with my friend.

The thought of him and her laying up, having sex made me wanted to cry or when I think about all those times she was texting him. He would say she was asking advice on her husband as to what to get him, I bought it. He fed me bullshit because he was too feeble of a man to admit he wanted it all. He knew I wasn't going to love him as I should if I knew the truth, but who knows. I still love him, but I had to love me. The weak woman I used to be was in a grave.

The day I discovered his lying was the day I wanted to die again. The only reason I was still standing was because of my children. They were my life support to my dying body. For them, I unplug the cord and woke up.

CHAPTER 4

We picked up the girls and fed them. From all their chattering, I took it they enjoyed their day, and I was glad. After what we have been through, they need a reason to be happy. The insurance company told me about the nonpayment, which I already knew it. I just waited until they came at me with it. Lending Hands holds our deed, and they charged it off because I was on a fixed income and Cedric's name was never on the deed.

I told Tammy and she told me I can get the cash I already have in it to buy me another place. I had never thought of that. They told me it'll be another week or so before they send me the cash value of ten thousand dollars. I gave them Tammy's address and they are going to send it. My cousin told me that she will be back at work, but on her next day off we could go looking for a place. In the meanwhile, I searched the web for listings.

It was me time as I put the girls in the bed. I am glad because I don't want them to see their dad. I know it sounds horrible but to me he didn't love them enough to be here for them. I was so thankful Lyn wasn't attached to him, but she cried for him more than I have. I don't like hearing her cry for her absent father, but she loves him, and sadly so do I. Time was getting away as I took a bath and put on some of the new clothes. The perfume was a plus and I was glad Tammy was gone out with a gentleman for the night.

I heard Cedric pull up and I got nervous all over. Tammy's last words were, keep him at arms distance. I wiped my hands on my revealing sun dress. I walked over to the door and asked, "Who is it?"

"Your husband."

"Sir my husband lives with another woman."

"Angela open up, it's me, Cedric."

I opened the door, smelling good and looking even better was Cedric. I was surprised because he handed me a rose, and said, "I know you love them, so I brought you one."

"Thank you," I spoke as I put the petals to my nose to sniff.

He came in and soon as I closed the door, he swoops me off my feet and stared into my eyes. I could not move even if I wanted to. He knew how to get to me as he held me in the air in his arms. The moment felt right and real. It was like, him doing what he did never happened, but I knew it had. He spoke above a whisper, "You are more beautiful, Angela, then I remembered."

"Thank you. Now put me down," I spoke as I found my voice.

"You are so right in my arms, and I don't want to put you down."

"Please," I insisted with a nervous tone. He released me slowly and I walked away the way Tammy told me to. I sat down and he was still standing and looking at me. I questioned once, "What is it?"

"You. You have changed on me."

"No, I always been this way you just never took the time to polish me up." We were quiet as I said, "Why won't you sit down?"

"Thank you."

He's being courteous, I thought. Cedric took a seat opposite of me, and said, "I've gone on with my life now and I have to stay away from you."

"Fine, but what about the girls? You haven't seen them in weeks. Don't you miss them?"

"You know I do."

"No, I don't. You don't act like a father who misses his girls."

"Right now, let's talk about us."

"What about us? You just told me you need to stay away from me because you have gone on with your life."

"I can't keep my eyes off you. Have you always been this amazing?" Cedric spoke in such a way that he knows I like.

"Yes, I have. Now keep your eyes close."

Cedric smiled, and said, "You've developed a sense of humor, too."

"It's always been there you just never took the time for it." My husband was quiet, and I knew it meant he thought of a way to ask me something, so he looked up at me and twirled his thumbs. *Yup he's nervous* I thought to myself as I spoke, "Out with it Cedric."

He gave me a smile, and said, "When I get situated, I want to bring the girls around Emma."

The look on his face told me he was serious, but I didn't care as I called out, "No and a hell fuck no!"

"Why not? You know she won't harm them. You know her and you know she is not a bad person."

"She harmed them when she helped destroy their parent's marriage. That qualifies her to be bad in my book."

"It could have been someone else and not her."

"I would rather it was another woman than a woman I called my friend. She has been in my house, and we have talked all the time about life. Now I know she has my husband, my children's father. How do you think I am to take that?"

"You are just hurt, but you'll get over it with a little time."

"Why didn't you let me in on how bad our marriage was?"

He stared at me and finally replied, "I loved you, but somehow, I fell out of love with you. I was afraid to let you know how I felt because I knew how you felt. I am not bad. I do care about you I just don't know how to take a woman like you."

"Meaning?"

"You are what any man in their right man would want. I don't get it why I don't want it right now."

"It's because you want a hoe life that she can give."

He gave me an all too familiar giggle as he spoke, "You will do anything in your power to help me, but I refuse it. I want to say, you are too much of a grown up for me and I still want to be me and playhouse."

"Yeah, playing house to a bitch that won't give you a home."

"I guess that could be it."

"You were playing when you met me?" I asked for I much needed to know how he was thinking.

"No. I was honest with you. I just woke up and decided I didn't want to be a family man anymore. I know it's wrong and not fair to you all, but its' how I feel, and I can't change it."

"How long were you aware of these feelings? I mean you tricked me. You really had me fooled."

"I had the feelings for some time. I was going to tell you when we talked about you adopting Lyn with me, but things kept happening to us then you got pregnant with Rossi, and I couldn't do it. The time never seemed right."

"Basically, when we got married you knew then?"

"Not then, but shortly after then. Angela no matter what kind of man I am, you are a keeper, and I wanted to keep you in my life."

"You should have asked me if I want to be the holdup of you not being you or getting your life together without us. I mean I am the reason you've acted like you were happily married all this time. What gives now?"

"You always have been right. I am holding you back because you have so much to offer another man."

"But it is you, my heart loves."

"And it pains me to hurt you as I have."

I was hurting now. Cedric said, "I signed the child support paper."

"Thanks."

I glanced over at him, and I knew he was about to say something funny when he said, "When you get the two hundred and fifty dollars, call me so you can give it back."

I couldn't even laugh as I turned my head and dropped it. He got up and sat next to me. Cedric lifted my hands and kissed them tenderly as he said, "Every time I see your face, I love to see a smile."

Under his spell, I was as I heard myself screaming but heard no words. I faced him as he leaned in to kiss me. I kissed him back. It was something about the way we were acting like teenagers. Every sense in my body yarned for him. Cedric placed timeless kisses on my arms and breast. He was allowing my body to reach for what he has to offer.

We were quiet as he said, "Would you make love to me for old time's sake?"

"If I hadn't seen it with my two eyes, I might have said yes, but knowing what I know now, no."

He got up with a little attitude, but I didn't care. I almost fell for him. I fixed my clothes and spoke with an oath, "Cedric, you were the only man my heart has ever loved and longed for. I gave you all my love. I poured my life into you and the children, and you didn't care enough to be honest with me. You took me for granted and tonight you had hopes that I would do what?"

"I don't know. I came home and become conscious of being with you was not what I wanted."

"What about the girls?"

66

"It's not fair to them if I stayed. I would make a lousy dad because I didn't want to have children so soon, but I love them. After Lyn's mom left me with her and you came along, I thought being a family man was the answer to my prayers."

It was as I could see clearly. No more fog. No more clouds. No more rain. I got up and began walking towards the door as I spoke, "You need to go. I have to start my life without you for them."

He stood up, and said with no pulse, "I came here to tell you that I want a divorce."

I ran up to his face, and replied harshly, "You just wanted to sleep with me one last time and now you talk about a divorce when I won't give it to you again."

"Your love making is timeless, Angela. No woman has ever made me feel the way you have. Sex is not the problem with us, it never was. It's me not wanting a family, the responsibility that come it. Sure, I would love to still sleep with you anytime you need me, but I know you would not approve."

"Before you sleep with me, I'll sleep with me."

I dropped my head, and he came over to me and sat beside me. I didn't move, but I knew it was coming, but didn't want to believe it. I held my head up and smiled cunningly. He moved back from me some as I said, "I almost cried, but I realized I have been a fool too long. You don't deserve me, or the girls and it took you leaving for me to see you don't need the family. Your best out is to hope you've made the right decision. So, don't try to catch me when I fall back, You should have been catching me when I was falling. I will see a lawyer and I am suing for full custody. With a new lifestyle children will cramp yours. Now get out and don't worry about us on this end. We going to be fine."

"Angela, I would do anything in the world for you if I can."

"There is something you can do for me."

"What's that?"

With a teary voice and the Spirit of fury all over me, I commanded my mind to make my mouth say, "Do my heart a favor and stay the hell out of it because if you don't leave as fast as you can right now, I might not be able to change my mind about killing you for making me feel the way I do about you."

Cedric stared at me and walked to the door fast. He stopped for a second, but he thought about what I said as he walked out the door. I politely closed the door and leaned on it. My mouth open as I stood with my back on the front door in disbelief. *What did I think was supposed to have happened tonight by him coming by?* I thought as I went to the steps to fold my hands-on top of my knees. I placed my head-on top of them. I don't know where my mind was, but I was lost in thought.

For all it was worth, I could not think of anything I could have or would have done to prevent this nightmare from occurring. I've put up a great show in front of Tammy and to myself, but it is when I am alone is when I am in agony. My heart aches for the love I assumed I had with Cedric. I feel lost without him. *How can you love someone so much and get on with your life in the same life? Maybe if it were just me it would be more manageable, but I have two wonderful little girls who may want their daddy as much as their mommy does. This man I adored and cared for does not feel the same. He says he did, but when he noticed that I wasn't what he wanted he didn't tell me. He continued to fool me.*

He went on to let me be his puppet and that is exactly what it was. I was on his string because he had me. He didn't have to worry or wonder about me. He knew I was his. He could have left me in a room full of eye candy men and I would still see him. I was never tempted because Cedric was all I could ever want. I'm glad all of this has happened earlier and not later or with more children. My goal is not only to get on with my life, but to learn how to live the kind of life Cedric threw his family away for.

I got up and sat on the couch as I kept refusing to cry. My nerves shook and my heart was overwhelmed with grief of loving a man that I shouldn't. A little while later, Tammy came in and she saw me. I saw her and that was all it took. I dropped my head. Words were not needed as she gave me a hug and a shoulder to lean on. I cried. I kept hearing her tell me to let it all out and how it's going to be ok. I really did want to have faith, but it is unbearable. The pain in my chest wouldn't let my heart go. I cried as if I heard some terrible news. It made no sense in the way the tears decided to come.

I knew my marriage could be over, but I didn't want to think of it as over. Somewhere in time, in part I hoped I had made a mistake about all I've gone through. For the better part, I had taken my time to fall in love and to be the mirror wife I had seen my grandmother be. Tammy spoke in my ear, "Just cry and get it out your system. Focus on discovering the real Angela. Let her come forth as the provider for her children and for herself. Let this Angela know she can't keep crying over the same thing. I have faith in you. I know you can weather this storm even through throwing hail. Angela, you can do it."

I sniffled a little and Tammy said, "Don't be the worried bitch, let that bitch Cedric be the worrying bitch. You have the wrong C in your vocabulary. Your C stands for Confident, Courageous and Careful. This day forward the C

70

will no longer stand for that thing that has left you in this condition. Do you hear me?"

"Yes, I do," I spoke with sniffles.

"Good now dry your face." I dried my eyes as Tammy said, "I knew you would break down after seeing him."

"You did?"

"Yeah, I did. I know we all are different, but it's something about when a woman loves. You my dear cousin loves the ground the bastard walks on and that is fine, but it is no longer accepted because you are better than what you are now. Loving him has caused you to reevaluate yourself."

"I want to believe it and I do when I hear you tell me, but when I get alone that is when I have the hardest time. It's like I am lonely and only have my thoughts."

Tammy was quiet before speaking again, "It's gonna be like that until you get him out your system. As for now you past the first test by not giving in. You wanted too and I honestly thought you would do it."

"Really? You thought I was going to cave."

"Yeah, I thought you were going to cave like a sink hole on soft ground. Ange that's your husband and you would do anything he tells you if it would improve your family life and y'all relationship. It's normal. I failed a time or two before I let Andre's dad go completely. But, when I

71

did let him go, he wishes he had me back but shit nawl. If I keep going backwards, I can't go forwards. A dog that back track never treats."

"I never looked at it in that manner."

"Ange, you gonna have to do some heavy praying when you feel weak enough to call him and sleep with him. Temptation comes and it's up to you if you want to let him be with you and her. If that be the case, you should never leave him if you are settled for that type of life, but I know you."

"You do don't you. Why are you home?"

"Dinner was lovely. The company was great. He wasn't hot on the eyes, but with a little liquor in me, shit he was warming me up by the second. I started feeling him, but my pussy was already feeling him. I told him I got an itch he can scratch. He smiled a nice smile. I got up and he paid for the meal. We walked out to his car, and I told him I can't go home because you and your baby daddy were getting it on. I did not want to bother y'all. He asked where I want to go. I said take me to the hotel for the night if he was up to it. He readily paid for it. We go in the room, and I stripped off by doing a sex tease. Soon as I turned around, I saw how small he was, but it did not bother me, at first. I thought he must be going to make up for it when he pleases my hidden friend."

"Your hidden friend?"

"Ange, my pussy" Tammy said flatly.

"Oh" I said as I laughed.

She laughed and spoke more, "I thought he is about to eat some pussy, so I felt a little better. I got on the bed and slowly crawled towards him. He moved out the way as I lay on the bed. He turned toward me and was about to get on me. I put my hands up and said, "What the hell you about to do?" He said, "Get on top of you and please you." I said no, "You gonna lick it first." He looked puzzled at first, but he scooted down between my legs. I arched my back, opened my legs all the way up for the first taste. He got down there and started gnawing on me. My first thought was, *what the fuck is he trying to do?* The more he gnawed here and there it came to me he did not know what to do or how to do it. I said to myself *you got your pussy all worked up for mother fucker who doesn't know what to do.* I glanced at the top of his head and decided he is wasting me and my pussy time. I took a deep breath and said aloud, "Fuck this shit." I moved some and said to him, "Get up for a minute." He lifted his head up at me. He had pussy juice all over his mouth and up his nose, another turn off. Again, I said, "Move out the way." He got out of my way. I got up and put my clothes back on. He kept looking at me before he asked, "What you doing? I wasn't finished." I stared back at him and said, "You ate me

73

out the mood for you." Girl, I left so quick. Shit, I could have played with myself and had a better time."

I laughed. Standing to my feet I spoke as serious as I could with a hint of giggles, "Tonight I stand before you as a witness of the passing of dear old pillar of the community, Mrs. Angela Shontae Myers-Hudson. She was a caring, loyal, faithful, humble, sincere, and honest, loving individual who did all she could in the flesh."

Tammy began laughing as I said, "Shush I'm having a funeral."

"Ok I will be quiet," Tammy said with a sly smile.

"Where was I?"

"All those caring words." Tammy pointed out.

"Yeah. She was all those caring words and then some. Her beautiful existence was cut short by life and a cheating, lying, no good, weak ass bastard who killed the sweet and innocent her. There is nothing to be done now because dear old Angela Shontae Myers-Hudson is gone on to be with the Lord."

I picked up the rose Cedric brought me as Tammy tried to hide her laughter. I took layers off the rose one by one and wad them in my right hand. I lifted them high, and said, "Here in my hand is the old good hearted, peacemaking, kind, sweet, generous"

Tammy interrupted me and said, "All those kind words?"

Laughing, I said, "Ma'am, we are almost finished, and I haven't asked for any remarks yet."

Tammy sat back and laughed. I continued. "R.I.P. to the old and hello to the new resurrected Angela Money-Maker Hudson. Now are there any final words from the audience?"

I sat down and Tammy stood up and tried to put on a straight face when she said, "I hope the old Angela discovers what she needs in her new world and how it is right before her eyes. Nothing more at this time, thank you Mistress of Ceremony."

I got up as Tammy sat down. Using a smile, I stated, "We had her funeral by tearing Angela Shontae Hudson-Myers to pieces. I will take her ashes and pour them out in the toilet."

Tammy jumped up shouting and being tickled when she yelled out, "That's what I'm talking about. Spread that bitch out so she can't come back, hell I've watched too many scary movies."

I giggled some more as I stated, "Sure will. Good night, girl."

"Good night and I liked the funeral. I didn't even want to cry."

"Bye, girl."

"Bye, Ange."

I laughed and went upstairs where my girls were and reality set in. I just had the funeral and all, but this ache in the middle of my chest snatched me again. I went to the toilet and flushed the wadded up rose petals down the toilet. The way the water looped made me compare my life and how it was calm on the surface. It's underneath that can suction you and pull you in a direction you may be unaware of.

Things happened and now everything was going around and around until it was no more. For the first time, I made up my mind. If Cedric wants a divorce, I will go on and give it to him. Leaving out the bathroom, I put on a gown and watch them sleep peacefully. They are my world and now I have to make their world is a happier one at all costs. I made up my mind for real about crying. I am tired of doing it. I feel like I have been crying by myself, but I know from what I have heard God sees our tears and hears our cries. He knows I did all I could do to save the marriage, but I could not do it alone.

The gospel song, "God Kept Me" was right on time for me. It played over and over in my head. I even closed my eyes to allow the words to sink into my soul. Yes, I had wanted to give up and let go. *I am so in love with the man I married, and it should be a crime to love someone so much and so hard. I have been depressed and sad when I am alone. No one not even Tammy knows how I am really dealing with all this. I know she cannot fully understand what I am going through, but she tries. It's hard enough just for me, but to have children to depend on me is another. It hurts even more because I haven't heard from my church family.*

The church is supposed to come looking for the lost sheep that hasn't been in a minute. There is no telling what I am dealing with or what anyone who quits going to church is dealing with, yet no one showed up. I was disappointed because for three years, I dedicated myself to the ministry, paid tithes, went to service faithfully, did whatever they asked of me, and there I was homeless, almost penniless until the first, and in need if spiritual guidance and fleshly understanding.

If the church doesn't take you in, the world will, and I don't want to be worse off than I was three years ago. Some of me wanted to end it all, but I knew they need me. I need me and if no one needs me, I knew God needed me. I went over to the balcony doors and began to stare outside. I saw how bright the moon was shining, and I remembered how light still shines in the dark and how Jesus is not unrighteous. HE will see me through this, I just must have faith and keep believing even when I don't feel like I don't have anything. If I stop right now, I will fall to pieces and not be any good. Lyn and Rossi need a strong mother to make it through this time. I have to be the example they need to see. Then, I thought about Tammy.

My cousin means well, but she is of the world and right now, she has been there to help me and my children during our earthly time of need. I cannot allow her to influence me to become something I am not; although, she knows how the world works because she was a part of it. I need Christ now more than ever. I need to be strong and happy, but I can't if I keep this heartache up. I knew when I stop crying, he better get scared. When I stop caring about him like I have, it's over.

I would be the one who got away from my husband. I was the one who had a change of heart and put my chips all in against him. As for this day, I am finished with him. Cedric won't be able to hit me with a red apple even if the target was on lock. My heart better get with the program and stop acting up in my chest when she feels like being loved. For I have come to learn if you want to make Boss moves, you have to hang with Boss players.

CHAPTER 5

The next day, Andre came home from Spring break and immediately got accepted to the School of Arts. He would be gone for the rest of the term and return at the end of the next school year. Tammy was sad about it but knows it is best for him. I was dragging my feet, but I realized that Cedric hasn't placed his life on hold and neither should I anymore.

However, the next twenty weeks flew by, and I hadn't had any meaningful conversations with any of the online men. They mostly want to play games, and I don't have time. Some even wanted me to pay their bills. I laughed. Many of the jokers had wives or a significant other. I cannot get tangled up in their mess while I am sorting through mine. Although, it becomes challenging. It gets lonely at night and even in the day. Everybody wants someone to hold and love and I am no different.

When the urge to have, sex crosses my mind, I would pray, and the good sensation would leave. Most of the time I would read the KJV Bible and read until I felt content in not giving in to call Cedric. Tammy told me when the girls go to sleep, to get the juice out me. I did it once and for some reason I could not bring myself to do it again. *I want something real and as long as I keep the fake, I can't get the real,* I thought. All this flirting and time wasting was useless.

79

On a brighter note, I hadn't heard from Cedric. I wasn't crying over him as much and I wasn't thinking of him as I thought I would have been.

The girls were consuming me more with them growing and being happy. I even found a place, but I was nervous because it didn't tell much about the house of the owner. I plan to see it soon. Nevertheless, to occupy my mind, Tammy and I would go out from time to time. I felt like a square in her circle. Men would come at me, but I didn't like their vibe so I next them. It was like something was keeping me from getting involved and half of me knew it was because I was already involved.

I have to get rid of this baggage before I could get the new and improved luggage. I've been out on dates and each one ended in a disaster. Luckily, Tammy would be close by to bail me out. There have been instances when they would come and I have a change of mind, Tammy would go in my place because she either knows of them or has dated a friend of theirs. On this evening after church, I lay there awake in a dreaming state. *It was like I was pretending to be something I was not. Going out on Saturday nights and church on Sunday's was old. I knew I couldn't have it like I want, but what was the harm of wanting.*

I would rather spend my Saturday nights cuddled up or spending time with a man who wants me for me and on

Sunday's we would get ready for church as a family. I don't want to keep wondering where I stood in my own marriage. I needed to stop delaying my divorce in hopes Cedric opened his eyes. The stuff I went through was like a girlfriend boyfriend relationship. When you get married it should be for life with the one you been waiting on all your life.

Cedric made the theory a lie for me. However, I would not let him destroy my identity of marriage. I don't know or understand the purpose of my life and how what I have gone through and in some form still went through. I must trust God and HIS plan, but I must still be faithful to the fact that Jesus loves me. I still believe in love and doing right in this wrong world. I closed my eyes and went to sleep empty.

The next morning, I woke up to a lot of in boxes from many different men. It was like it all happened overnight in an instant. I was nervous and excited, but emotionally drained. The girls were still asleep as I went downstairs to Tammy's room. I knocked and she was up getting ready for work. I opened the door and spoke, "I have a lot of in boxes and since I prayed last night they are coming left and right."

"Girl let me see."

I handed her my phone and she said, "Look at this one."

She showed me the picture and it was Henry Darling. We both looked at each other. I had never thought Henry would be contacting me and here he is. I became a little excited as she asked, "Aren't you going to reply?"

"I don't know. We been friends and for him to be in my in box screams something different."

"Why not? It is the perfect one?"

I laughed as I said again, "I don't know."

"Think about it. You already know things about him, you have had conversations with him, and you know he is a real man who is not ugly at all, and I bet his dick has a curve."

"How can you tell just by looking at him?"

"He looks like he has an unusual dick that will make a girl go crazy. Just look at him."

She showed me his picture again as I stated, "This is the first time I am really seeing him in another light."

"He always looked like this?"

"I guess so."

"He is a turn on, Ange, and if you don't want to talk to him, me and my girls will talk to him and have a damn good conversation with him."

I smiled as she said, "How many of those other guys do you know are really a real man that is as fine as he is?" I shook my head no. She said, "At least you'll be on the same playing field with Cedric."

"Yeah, but I don't want it to look like we just swapped out."

"This is the world, and we don't care what things look like. Remember the old Angela passed away few weeks ago so stop resurrecting her. Get out your feelings."

"She did, didn't she?"

"Give him a shout out and meet him for lunch. The girls will be at the daycare, so you have all day. Who knows you might get what you been long overdue for."

"Bye Tammy and go on to work," I spoke as I laughed and threw my hand up at her.

About twenty minutes later, I heard Tammy go out the front door to work. I inbox him back and told him I would like to take my time and communicate through Facebook. I want to be more comfortable and not discuss our spouse's. He said he understood; therefore, our friendship began by texting and phone calls. After talking secretly with Henry for weeks, I decided it was time to meet in person and ask him out like Tammy suggested way back then. I texted him and asked if he would like to meet for lunch. He responded back extremely fast to say yes. I was scared, but here I am excited about seeing a man I have known. Even though, Henry is not just any man. He is the husband of the woman that has my husband. Other than that, he is really a descent looking, nice, hardworking man with no children.

For the most he was always pleasant to be around. I would like to know his side of this twisted story. I checked my phone and saw it was almost seven fifteen. Quickly before the girls got up, I bathed and decided to put on a nice dress and sandals. I got the girls up and took them a bath. We all were headed downstairs as Lyn asked, "Where daddy?"

"Daddy," Rossi repeated happily.

"Mommy where daddy?" Lyn asked again.

"Where daddy?" Rossi repeated after her sister.

I could tell them he is on a long business trip, but I would not make the habit of lying to them. I would tell them the truth; although, they may not understand it. When we reached the bottom of the stairs, I spoke as I directed them to the kitchen to eat, "Daddy is gone and it's gonna be just us girls for a while. Is that, ok?"

"Okay," Lyn said.

Rossi repeated, "Ok."

"Good, eat so we can get you off to Daycare."

They both hollered out yay as they began to eat the cereal I placed before them. I gave the text another look over and began smiling and I don't know why. There I was about to get on the road of no return, and I liked it. I got up and cleaned up the few dishes, put the girls in the stroller, and headed off to the daycare. There was a skip in my step and joy in my skin. I did not know what to expect from meeting Henry as we made it to the daycare. The girls were eagerly jumping as I signed them in at the office. I took them to their different classes and signed them in there.

On my way out, I considered how different men were watching me. My eyes rolled to look at my left hand for them to see I am married. When I glanced down myself it had no ring. It has been a while since I wore it and had forgotten about it. For it is a natural reflex to show off your ring. I grinned some and kept going. I can say I have spent more time in this married relationship than I have unmarried in this brief time. I took my time and walked to the park.

I saw a spot, which seemed reserved just for me. The small bench seat was surrounded by concrete. Trees made the perfect shade as the wind blew silently. I sat there and could hear the birds chirping. I thought *if Our Father in heaven can take care of the needs of small birds, what I am? They don't even work for survival and yet they eat, and they live. If HE is doing that for them, I know confidently HE will do that for me, now more than ever.* I had no idea where that came from as I looked around and felt awkward. My phone vibrated and Henry was calling me off Facebook. I answered, "Hello."

"Hi Angela."

His voice was hypnotic. An awkward feeling crossed me as I replied softly, "How are you, Henry?"

"I am great. I am going to walk to the restaurant today because it is beautiful."

I didn't know what to think because I had looked forward in seeing him again. In fact, any male interaction at this point would be charming. Making sure my voice was I replied, "It is a beautiful day, and I am enjoying this day as we speak."

"From this view, it is more captivating that I ever imagined."

He was quiet as he said, "See ya, Angela."

"Okay. Bye, Henry."

I hung up and started going through my inboxes and checking my pages. I began to play around with my phone as I heard a voice requesting an answer, "Angela, wow."

I looked up and became entranced by a wonderful smile and a pair of warm eyes. It was Henry. He was taller than I imagined, and I could smell him from here. His hands were huge, and he does have the sex appeal that makes a girl like me want to give it up. I gathered myself so he could hear me say, "Wow?"

"Yes, you look amazing."

"Thank you."

"I thought that was you when I called. I had to see if it were really you. When you picked up, I became at a loss for words."

"Really, Henry?"

"Yes, I did not recognize who you were. You look amazingly different."

"Amazingly different?"

"Not that anything was ever wrong with you before, but you look simply astonishing."

He paused before saying, "Wow. You have demobilized my eyes from the nature scene because of your presence alone captures my very attention."

"Thank you. Henry, you don't look bad yourself. Won't you sit down?"

I scooted over a little and smelled his cologne even stronger before he sat down. It is eight thirty in the morning and I was shuttering at the scent of a man. My own husband never smelled that good before. Henry smiled, and said, "I got a place not too far from here and most of the time I work from home. This park is the only place I can go to as for being close to nature. Sometimes, when I come out here, I end up staying for hours at a time."

We were quiet as I tried to break the awkwardness by saying, "My girls are enrolled in the daycare down the street, and we've been living at Tammy's since the house fire."

"Yeah, I heard about the fire. I wanted to reach out but decided to wait. You got what you need, or you need anything?"

"It's coming."

"If you need anything more let me know. I don't mind helping you out."

"Thank you."

"You're welcome."

There was an uncomfortable silence. I mean we have talked, but that day our conversation seemed to be more. He acted like he has things on his mind. I hadn't been in the game like that in over four years and being married but living single for weeks. We looked at each other and turned our heads. He asked, "What do you do for a living? I couldn't remember, but I know it was something with lawyers."

"I did. I used to be a Paralegal until my accident."

"I knew it was something along those lines."

"Yup a paralegal. What do you do, now?"

He flashed that smile to say, "In my spare time, which I love doing, I design websites and set up various things for many people. In the real world, I am a supervisor over security systems throughout this school district."

"Your job sounds like a job."

"It is. Sometimes it is hectic. You have to make sure people come to work on time and they are doing their job to protect the children. You can be nice to the children, but you cannot have unhealthy relationships when your job is on the line. Although, you can get a headache from it, the position pays very well, and I won't complain about it. I just take two BC's and call it the day."

I laughed as I stated, "Must be nice to have BC's to solve your problem."

"Sounds nice," he said with a smile. Henry said as if he were in a dream world, "It does sound nice to be able to work on things you love, so what would you like to work on?"

Feeling humorous I stated, "Other than this life of mine?"

"Other than this life of ours, you mean," Henry added with a laugh.

"I would love to design weddings for people. Those moments are supposed to last a lifetime, and I want to be in on happiness. I want to almost guarantee their special day would be as memorable as the day it happened. When they look back at the pictures."

"Hopeless romantic?" Henry asked in a whisper.

"Plus, I do not have to be still. Since my accident, my back acts up a lot when I am not moving for a long time. Sometimes in the mornings it hurts me to put my shoes on."

"As for the pain, back surgery may help to relieve some of the discomfort" he added.

"The doctor has told me if it gets worse surgery would be the last alternative, but he won't recommend it unless he just has to."

We both were quiet again as he said, "Don't you want to finally talk about your husband and my wife? I know I do."

I was off guard for real. I said using humor, "Since you opened the bag of worms, I mean cheaters. Yes, it came across my mind when I saw your inbox. It was different and I knew it must be something. I didn't know if you inbox me for some type of scoop or you inbox me because you are interested in talking to me."

"I am interested in you as a person. I had inbox you, for enjoyable conversation because you always had that peace about you. Other than I know you and I don't know any of the other women in my inbox."

We both laughed as I said, "Tammy and I were saying the same thing this morning. She told me how I know you and everything. Since you opened the door, you can go first or me?"

"I will," Henry said as I slanted my body in a position where I was able to see his entire body language and facial expressions.

He tilted his head as to remember when he said, "Uh let's see. Emma left me after being married for a year. She said I was boring living the ordinary life. I asked her about her happiness, and she said she was happier with me before the marriage. I tried telling her in a marriage there is only one business and not two, but she wasn't listening. She's wild and I don't know if age played a part in it or what."

"It did. Cedric is a year younger than me, but younger is still younger. I'm sure you already know that."

"Emma is in her early twenties while I am thirty-nine."

"I guess age can't be it because Cedric is with me in age. It must be the excitement."

He laughed and said, "Probably. Nevertheless, she said she had changed from the Emma I met. One day she left her phone, and a man called her. Seeing the number prompted me not to trust her. I would go through her phone and see countless messages from other men on social media. She even had porn coming to her phone daily. She would say many things and I would buy it until I kept seeing your number show up on my phone bill."

"Cedric phone was in my name. His credit is bad, but mine isn't."

"Same with me. Her phone was in my name because her credit is too poor; therefore, I was allowed access to the numbers being called or texted."

"I see we have some things in common," I spoke with a small smile.

"Your smile is an automatic showstopper. I'm sorry am I too forward?"

"You good and we are grown. Thank you for the compliment," I replied with ease.

"The truth doesn't need a compliment."

I didn't know what to think as I liked the man in my presence. This man removed doubt from my mind with his words. Henry said, "I thought I loved her, but when she began to take, it became a red flag. She never cooked and cleaned. Sex was second to none and I didn't know what to do. I've asked her to get help or at least consider getting marriage counseling with me, but she turned them down. She was always busy, on the move, doing nothing. She didn't work. She didn't have to. She spent all her time with other people, gambling at the Casinos, and splurging the money. If she hadn't left, I might not have been able to bounce back like I did."

"She won't have that problem with Cedric because he doesn't have a lot of money. He passed his police exam. Until then, he worked as the janitor at the elementary school. I don't know if he is still there because he said he wasn't. It could be a ploy for me not to ask him for money."

"How are the girls, anyway, if you don't mind me asking?"

"I don't mind. They are great and thank you for asking. They are growing like weeds and asking for their daddy every so often."

I became solemn as he changed the awkwardness by saying, "The last time I saw them was about a year ago when I ran into you and them at the grocery store."

"Yes, it was. We were picking up some groceries and don't you know when I got to the counter, it said my card didn't have any money on it?"

"Wow."

"I was stunned because I didn't go anywhere and didn't know how it all happened. I called the card, and they said my funds were on there, but someone took them off. I had no idea Cedric had another card sent. Of course, he claimed he didn't know what happened to it."

"What you do?"

"I had to leave the things at the counter. The girls were crying for the things I was going to buy for them. I was embarrassed and stunned."

"I could only imagine your feelings, but if I had known I would have bought them for you."

"The day he left; don't you know he said you act like you don't see this shit unfolding? Henry, I didn't. I really didn't see it or us coming a part. I was too caught up in doing right that him doing wrong was my last choice. So many nights I would cry and so many nights he wouldn't be there to comfort me. I didn't think anything was wrong because he was always busy. I really thought he was happy. I knew I was happy, and the girls were happy. He came home and took everything, but the kitchen sink."

I was solemn as I looked away. Henry scooted closer and I laid my head on his shoulder. It felt right as I wanted to cry but fuck it. Crying over Cedric was the last thing I needed to do. Henry said loud enough for me to hear, "Emma and I were separated, and then in the process of getting a no-fault divorce."

"Do you want one?" I had to ask as I lifted my head up.

"Yes. You can't get wasted time back. Emma and I did the time wasting along with energy. I thought I loved her, but I was infatuated with here and she was in love with the

94

money I made and the things we did with people that being with just me was a no-no."

"How long did you date?"

"A few weeks before getting married."

"Kind of rushed it, huh?"

"I did, but I thought she was the one."

We were silent again as I sparred, "When our own child came along, he quit talking to me. When he did talk to me he only complained about the house and how he was fed up with us not having all we needed. He failed to realize I would have stayed in a shed with him as long as we were happy. Not having the finer things in life was never a biggie with me. Love, peace, happiness, and good will towards my fellow man meant a lot to me. Don't get me wrong it would be nice to go somewhere and not worry about the price or if an emergency came up. I could go to the place or pay for whatever it was. I'm saying, being happy in a home is better than being well to do in a house any day. Each time I tried telling Cedric, he acted like he did not understand what I was saying. He would rather take his friends out than to take me. When he gets mad at me, he can be some kind of ugly, and it hurts. My husband was good to everybody, but me. He even accused me of being too busy because I had the girls all the time and no time for him. He didn't try to help me with them; he only complained about them. I took it as his excuse to put all the responsibility off on me while he went scot-free. He didn't have to worry about anything because if my credit couldn't get, I borrowed or used my work check before my accident. What more was it for me to do if I have been doing it all?"

"You did right, and you have done more than the average woman. If a man complains about his family there is nothing you can do, but to let him go. Let him see how it really is to not have his family."

I dropped my head some when I said, "Cedric probably wouldn't notice any difference. He'll be busy celebrating with not a care in a world."

"You think?"

"Yes, I do. Anytime he complained about the help he did I could only imagine what he would do if I wasn't working to do it or if my disability check couldn't get it?"

"Angela, you think he wouldn't notice, but he would. It is the small things like coming home to lay beside the person who loves you or will do anything for you. It's eating a hot breakfast being cooked in love or sharing a laugh or two. It's when you feel like you are alone, but you are not because someone has your back. Angela, it is the small things from putting on his socks, to giving him his medicine that means so much and, it's the smallest things that breaks up a home."

"You make marriage sound so happily ever after, Henry."

"It's supposed to be even if it doesn't turn out what you want the first time around."

"It does, but in my case it didn't. Don't you know he took the tissue, soap, can food, sugar, opened pint of milk, and meat?"

Henry seemed like he got mad as he exploded, "What kind of sick bastard would do that to his wife and kids!"

I was shocked by his response. He was genuinely stern with his words. To add salt to the situation I responded with bitterness, "Mine's did and he didn't think anything was wrong with it."

"Like hell it wasn't. You don't take from your wife and children. Your job as a real man is to protect them with all you have and then some. They are the last ones you cause havoc on. They will be there when you have no one in your corner."

He froze when he said those words. Henry took a moment and said softer, "I'm sorry. It made me angry because it was foolish and selfish of Cedric. Doesn't he know there are men out who would love to have a family or have a trusting woman to come home to? In this world, there are too many good women being treated like a mere girlfriend and too many sneaky women being treated like outstanding wives."

"I agree, but what else is there?"

"The thing is, there is so much out there, you have to want to see it and not be settled."

"You think that's what I was doing?"

"For now, I can't say that. I think you were doing what you supposed to for your family and got taken for granted in the process."

I liked the sound of that as I asked, "You would love to have a family, wouldn't you?"

"Yes. I love children. I grew up in a large household and there was always joy, arguments, and love. It was never boring."

"Cedric said I can have the children and to think of this as my get out of jail free card."

Henry rose up to say, "A get out of jail free card, and you can have the children?"

"They ask for him and I chose not to lie. I just said it's gonna be us for a while and they said OK."

"They are what four and two?"

"Exactly. Dig this tho he said he would make a lousy father if he had stayed with me. I asked him how long he felt this way and he said he had the feeling long before I had

Rossi." It actually pained me to speak those words aloud, but I did. Hearing it spoken, did not hurt as much as it used to.

Henry said, "I been knowing you for a little over five years and we were supposed to have been a set up by Tammy. Who was dating a cousin of mine, but my car broke down and we didn't meet again until you were pregnant with Rossi, right?"

"Yup. Fate has an odd way of coming into our lives."

"Who would have thought we supposed to have met all those years ago, but didn't until now? I say God had us to be in the marriages we were in to have us where HE wanted us to be at this time in our lives. I believe in crazy faith where you ask the Lord for something, and HE will grant it to you. Do you agree?"

"It sounds like it is the possible answer as for the agreeing for something like that maybe."

"Maybe?" he questioned back at me.

"Yes maybe. In today's world people do not reference Christ like they should and by that for them even for me, to believe that HE could do something like that does sound far out there."

"Maybe to you, but it seems like God is gonna have to do something out the box for you."

"He's gonna have to."

We were quiet. My first thought was *how people turn to religion when they are going through something, and I don't want to be like that. It hit me how Henry believes in a higher power.* To make sure, I asked, "You always been involved in church?"

"I wasn't until my brother had a wreck. That close call prompted me to believe in God more than I already did. You see, they expected my brother to die, but I prayed like it was my life on the line. When he pulled through, I knew it was Jesus that did it. Seeing him alive isn't something I heard, it was something I seen with my own eyes."

"How old were you?"

He dropped his head to say, "A little over a year ago. All of this happened about the time Emma left me. I was going through. I was trying to hold onto my wife, but once my brother pulled through, I told her I was done swinging and all that. I have done things I am not proud of, but I am human and all that were before I became the man I am now."

We were quiet as he asked, "Would you like to attend service with me?"

For him to ask me about service blew my mind. I got the courage to say, "What type of church is it?"

"Glad you ask. It's one where they speak in tongue. It's one that believes Jesus is God and how you have to have HIS Spirit by being born again."

"Oh ok."

"Is that a problem?"

"No. I wouldn't want to attend any other church. I would love too, but I am not going to bring the girls until I check it out for myself, but if Tammy isn't home, I will have to bring them."

"You supposed to go first. You can't just take your children to a service because it is a service. You don't know what all goes on at the service. I know Tammy is a free bird and you might have to bring them. If you do, we have older Mother's that keep the children while service is going on."

"That sounds great."

He smiled, and said, "Here I am asking you out and we haven't even made it out to lunch yet."

"It's ok. I didn't mind."

"You have that effect on me already. I can only imagine what we are in for."

I responded with a smile, "Who knows who knows?"

CHAPTER 6

Henry glanced at his watch and asked, "I'm ready to be served some food. You want to walk to the restaurant and not mentioned those two we married for now?"

"I would love to if you don't mind."

He got up and offered his elbow to me. I entwined my arms through the loop, and we began to walk. We talked about everything. When we got to Penn's we didn't eat much. We were too busy talking as if we were long lost friends. I hadn't enjoyed company like his in an exceedingly long time. Being out with him reminded me of my single days. We chatted about his life and mine. I couldn't believe how open and forward I was with him. I found myself telling him things my cousin never knew.

It was strange, but a good strange. I don't know if he was good company because he was not my husband or was simply good company in general. I know for sure I could be myself with him and I liked it. He even told me I was fun, and he could tell I am a sincere person. Henry was unbiased about things I said, and he would call himself giving me advice about life. For the most he was right. I would tell him what I thought about his situations, and he would listen.

I could see he was as surprised as I was about our closeness. I was surprised at the fact he and I were connecting. It wasn't personal because of our situation was similar, but different. This man in my presence was listening to me. He even laughed at the silly jokes I told. That was something Cedric had never done before. It came time for us to go. I didn't want to go, and I felt he didn't, either.

We enjoyed ourselves too much and there was no way it would end. He paid for our lunch, and we began to walk back towards the park arm and arm, not like lovers, but as great friends. I didn't feel guilty being out with him and enjoying his company. I was a woman in need of being treated like a woman and Henry did that to me. I didn't want to let him go, but I knew our day together would end. We finally made it back to the park bench. With gentleness and compassion Henry spoke sincerely, "I brought you back safely from your destination, Angela."

The way my name rolls off his lips made my toes curl in my sandals. His deep voice is a panty dropper, but I could not do it just yet. I could only stammer out, "Yes sir, you have, and I thank you for being such a gentleman in today's time." We laughed as I stated, "I'm usually not this forward, but I would like for you to have my number, if you want it."

I was nervous. There I was a grown woman who acted like a child in front of a gorgeous man. He made me feel comfortable and yet nervous. Henry smiled when he called out, "You are smart, funny, and beautiful. What man would not want your number?" With a smile, I dropped my head and shook it as I called out my number. He said with laughter, "Now, here is my personal cell number if you ever get stranded or need some help, call me. I will come running if I must. You can even text me if you want. If I see it, I will respond if my service is not whack."

"I would love it. This is my first phone, and I do not have anyone to text or call other than Tammy."

"Cedric doesn't have your number?"

"No. I don't want to give it to him because I don't think he deserves it."

"He doesn't, but you do have his children. Give it to him so he cannot ever throw it up in your face how he could never contact you all. A man like him could do that sly trick. Just because he has it, does not mean you have to answer it all the time if he calls."

"You right. I didn't think of it from the point of view you just made."

"If he has it and he doesn't ever call, it is on him. You did your part, unless you think he is going to stalk you or something," Henry spoke with ease.

"Doubt it."

"He doesn't know you are on the dating scene sort of speak. Once he sees it, he will. I am a man I know what I am talking about."

"Maybe just once you are wrong."

"He knows he has you and my soon to be ex-wife. Why not keep you both entertained with the notion of wanting one more than the other."

"He called Tammy's house phone a few weeks ago and nothing more was heard. He knows the number and hasn't used it. He even knows I am still at her place, but if you think it'll be a clever idea for him to have it, ok."

"I do. You have children even if he doesn't pull his part."

"Does Emma have your number?"

"She does, but she doesn't call."

"Not yet," I stated back to him in an assuring way.

"What makes you so sure?"

"You are out with me, and she thinks you will continue to sulk over her because you love her, and you were married."

"I am doing a lot better getting over her. I haven't been dating or anything. I need to get things squared away with her first before I can think of a relationship."

"I feel the same way."

"Yours is new with children, while she and I are at the end. We are just waiting to go to court to have the judge look over it."

"I'm telling you; she will try to stop it."

"I don't think so."

"What you want to bet?" I spoke coyly.

"What are you willing to bet?" Henry asked in a sexual way.

I caught the way he said that and so did my pussy. I smiled and said calmly, "What you willing to lose?"

He gave me a smile as he spoke kindly, "Anything you think you could gain by me losing."

"It's not fair."

"Why isn't it?"

"I don't know a whole lot about you other than meeting you a few times and casual conversations here and there."

"I guess you are going to have to see me more often before you can make a bet."

My heart skipped a beat. Out of all the times, I had ever talked to him, I never saw past his conversation, and I was not trying to see anything else, but there I was, looking at that man like a man and not a friend. I spoke with a question, "Are you implying we start seeing each other to make one of them jealous?"

He smiled at me and spoke as if he was closer to me than he appeared "No. I'm implying we start hanging out and finding out what it means to be a friend. Right now, we cannot offer each other any more than friendship. You are still in a marriage you may want to keep, and I am out of a marriage my wife did not want to keep. We both have trust issues and baggage to work on let alone work on ourselves. You have two little girls who do not need a man in and out of their lives until you are sure of the man or yourself. To go a little further, recognize how you feel about yourself and your life."

He made so much sense as I stated back to him, "I guess it is only right we spend time together and be a friend to the other. I mean there are things I can tell Tammy, but she doesn't really get it."

"She can't get it. She can only tell you her opinion and what she would do, but to really be one to go through it, is another story."

"I agree, but what makes you different?"

He moved closer to me as he said, "I am different because I have actually been there. I mean being married and hurt by the one you loved. I am a man, and I can tell you from a man's point of view. I can't speak for all men, but I can give you a general idea about what we as men think."

"I'll take the answer you gave."

"Angela, Tammy has never been married, but it doesn't mean she can't offer you the advice you look for. What I am saying is, because she has never been married, she can only tell you what or how she overcame in her relationship being single. She can only tell you from the world's point of view if her advice is the advice, you look for, but when you talk about a marriage it is a whole new level. She may not fully understand how you are good as long as people are around but when you are alone with your thoughts and memories you break down. It was not easy for me, and I can only imagine how it is for you with two small children involved. You just don't want to throw your marriage away because of one infidelity. Make sure this is what you want."

"He already asked for a divorce."

"Oh, but you still have to make sure if that is what YOU really want. Despite of what HE wants."

I could tell he was surprised. I wanted him to reassure me I could be wrong as I spoke with uncertainty, "I guess it is serious for him and her."

"Maybe, but is it what you want? If you want your husband, go after him with all you have, but if you want to give up because you had enough fine. However, you look at it. Angela, make sure it is a decision you can live with. You have grounds for divorce. He abandoned you and the girls. Not only that, but he has committed adultery and still is."

Closing my eyes, I stammered, "Do you want the truth?"

"I will have it no other way."

"I want things to go back the way they were. If I had a magic eraser, I would wipe out all the bad and redo anything I had done wrong to make this marriage go south. I deserve to be happy and it's not because I can make a man happy. I understand everyone doesn't cheat and things happen, but they don't keep happening, either. I want my girls to have their dad in their lives instead of him being absent. I want the unquestionably loyalty of what a marriage can bring because I know I can bring it to the table and if the need be like it is now. I learn how to eat alone."

"Even if means you're unhappy because if you are justly unhappy then you are only prolonging the inedible. It wouldn't be healthy for the girls to grow up in a home where the parents don't love each other as they should. You can't be in a marriage or a relationship because you have children. Many people get it mixed up. They hang in there because of the children and that's the biggest mistake. Children can prosper from two happy parents in two different households than two parents in one household who secretly hates the other."

"Is this from experience?"

"Yes. I found out when I graduated from high school my parents only stayed together because they had seven children. They were only together for us, and it made me upset because they probably missed out on their lives

109

because of us. It wasn't fair to them or us about our parents stayed married for the wrong reason."

"They stayed married for seven reasons" I spoke with humor.

Henry gave a small laugh as he spoke with confidence, "I vowed I would not base my reasons to stay like they did. When I have a family, I will stay devoted to my wife and if we are not happy, I will discuss it with her about the best choice. Cheating is never the answer."

"You are passionate about family and love. I can tell by the way you talk. I'm sure a lot of women would agree."

"Do something different" Henry suggested.

Those three words opened my eyes as I replied with joy, "I am. Being he wants a divorce, I'll go on and give it to him. No questions asked. Usually I would question all things, but not this time. Normally I would keep at him to make sure whatever the decision was the one he wanted. This time, I am going to let it ride with no questions because I don't want to keep a man who didn't want to be kept."

"He wants to be kept all right, but he wants to do him in the process. But are you ok with the rush decision? You do have children and most importantly you have you."

"I am not rushing my decision. I understand all you said. In fact, I have already thought about it all thoroughly. I don't want to be held responsible for someone wanting to get on with their lives and they cannot do it because of me. If Cedric is not happy, I don't want him in our lives because he would only make us miserable. The girls deserve better."

"Have you found a lawyer?"

"I really haven't looked. He asked for it a few and weeks, and weeks, and weeks ago. I decided to go on and give it to him. I've been putting it off in hopes things will change."

"They can't change if you don't."

Henry was right as usual. I hunched my shoulders and looked down. Henry used his hand to lift my head to say, "Don't ever drop your head. You have no need to worry or stress."

I didn't know what to say. He looked into my face as if to search for something. I broke the gaze by asking, "Why are you so confident?"

"It took a lot of counseling and perseverance, but I did it and so can you."

"Do you have a lawyer in mind?" I had to ask.

He let go of my face to take out his wallet. He handed me a card. I looked at it and Henry said, "This is my brother. He is a lawyer, and he is good. I am currently using him now."

"When will your divorce be final?"

"Next month to be exact the first."

"You filed so you both can go your own way and if it means to get this over with. I might as well file the same way, but with full custody and supervised visitations if the need be. Hopefully, I get my own place soon."

"Have you found a place to stay?"

"I found a place in the country about twenty minutes from here. I only saw the picture on the internet, and it doesn't tell a whole lot more. It has a big yard and it's a four bedroom with two bathrooms. It might be in my price range, which must be close to free."

"Where about exactly?"

"It's on North Cedar Rd."

"Oh. I know where you are talking about."

"Have you seen it?"

"I have and your girls will love it. Angela, you can also apply for HUD. They can help you in getting approved for a place."

"I don't want to rent."

"They can help with a place of your own as well. You have to find the place like the one you are talking about now."

"Oh ok."

"I can take you if you like."

Sounding excited, I spoke, "You would do that for me?"

"Why not? If I can help, I will."

"Thank you so much."

"I must go. You want me to walk you back to the daycare?"

"No. I'm going to stay here for a little longer."

"I'll call you later" he said.

"I'll look forward in hearing from you."

Henry picked up my other hand and kissed it. His lips were soft and the way they brushed against my skin caused sensations to flow all over me. I was beginning to shake some as he released my hand. Henry knows what he did to me as he smiled and walked off. I had to grab a seat and gather my senses. It makes no sense for him to arouse me like he does. I don't know if it's because I hadn't had a real man in a long time or just maybe it is real.

I continued to sit there and think about Henry. I never thought he and I would be hitting it off as good as we are. I took out my phone and text Tammy. I told her we have to talk when she gets home. She told me it'll be about seven. I was excited all over again as I got up to get the girls. Henry has brought me back to life and I know it is him and the conversations we have had thus far. Seeing Henry that day allowed us to be close. At night, I smiled more, as Cedric became a distant memory. Today, I drop the girls off and

Henry texted asking about church. I finally gave in and said yes.

The girls never want to leave daycare and that lets me know the place is doing something right. All while I pushed them towards Tammy's they chatted. It was like a hidden language only they understood because I didn't get it. My mind was on Henry and the smile he put on my face that day. We made it to the front door and went in. Soon as I opened the door, Cedric was waiting.

My mouth dropped. The girls hollered out, "Daddy!"

"Hey kiddos," Cedric spoke as if he just got off from work.

"What are you doing in here?"

"Tammy told me to go on in and wait."

The girls were all over him and I hated it because when he leaves, I am going to have two kicking and screaming children in need of their father. He walked over to the couch and sat back down with the girls sticking to him. I put the roller cart up and put their evening snack on their small table. I went back over to the other couch. He said, "Girls, get down and let me talk to your mom for a minute."

"You stay, daddy?" Lyn asked.

He cut them off by saying, "Let me talk to mommy. You girls go to your table and eat your snack mommy put out for you to eat."

The girls got down and went to their little table at the corner of the kitchen where I can see them. I faced him, and he said, "You look beautiful."

"Save the compliments. You never dished them out when I was with you so, please don't start."

He was coy as he spoke, "You are right. I let things overcome me."

"What do you want here?"

"I can't drop by and talk to my wife."

"No. State your claim and leave."

"I miss you that's all."

"Does Emma know you over here telling me how you miss me?"

"We aren't talking about Emma. We are talking about my wife," he said directly.

"What do you want?" I stated with a stern tone.

"Don't ask your husband a question if you don't want the answer."

He got up and I put my arms between us, and said, "Step back. I don't want nor need you too close to me."

"Are you afraid?"

"No, but I am going to give you the divorce you seek."

"You can wait. I just wanted to drop by to let you know I miss you and how I been thinking about you and us."

"Think about you and the wrong us."

"Is there another man?"

"Is there another woman? Wait. You do have another woman."

He stood close to me, and spoke, "Better not let me find out who he is because you're still my wife."

"Goodbye Cedric, and the next time call before you come by. I won't let you pop up when you feel the need."

"I need your cell and not this house number."

I called his phone as I went over to the door and opened it for him. He said, "May I say goodbye to the girls?"

"You said your goodbye when you left them asking after you for many weeks ago or was it the fire they burned up in?"

He stopped in front of me and made a motion to kiss me. I flexed and slapped him as hard as I could. He was in awe and so was I. He didn't get mad as he said, "I had that coming."

I didn't answer as I began closing the door with him in it. He moved out the way and left. I half-heartedly expected him to snatch me up, but he didn't. His tone didn't even change and that was a shocker. I locked the door and stood there still amazed how I hit him. My heart was hammering like never before. I made my way to my cell and text Tammy. I told her I slapped Cedric. She sent an emoji face with the mouth wide open.

The girls were quiet. I went to check on them and they both were laid over on their table asleep. That slightly made me smile. It really did something to my heart to see them in that way. First, I took Lyn upstairs to her side of the bed. I went back downstairs and got Rossi and placed her on her side. I took a shower and got in my evening clothes and house coat.

CHAPTER 7

I waited for Tammy, but she did not come in. I know she must be up to something. Finally, she did text me, saying she would stay the night with one of her men and she won't be coming in. *When am I going to talk to her about me slapping Cedric?* I thought as I decided to go on to bed.

The next morning, I got the girls up and ready for church. I wasn't going to take them, but Tammy wasn't here to keep them. The girls were excited about going to church. I told them a friend of the family was taking us because Mommy doesn't have a car. They were excited all the same as Henry pulled up and came to the door like a gentleman. The girls were distant, and I expected them to be as we locked them down in the car.

I got in and he drove off. He glanced over at me, and said, "You look beautiful this morning."

"Thank you for you is just as handsome yourself this day."

"It's the woman and children in my presence that makes me look the way I do."

I gave him a smile and made ware of my environment. I could see the church and the area screamed peace as he turned into the parking lot. We could hear the music from the car as we all got prepared to go in. The nervousness was setting in. I had a problem with the church because they didn't help me when I needed it the most. Henry glanced at me to say, "You ok. You act like you afraid."

"No. I'm just being cautious."

"That's a good thing."

Lyn asked, "We at our church mommy?"

"No baby. We are visiting this church."

"Ok."

"Ok" Rossi repeated.

We walked in and to my surprise the people did not look back at us. Normally when the doors open people tend to see who has come in, but that didn't happen. Henry led us to the fourth row of the small church. He let me in as I placed Rossi on my lap with Lyn sitting between us. As we sat down so did the choir. The Deacons stood up as the Ushers directed the people to drop in their tithes and offerings. I gave the girls a dollar each and Lyn asked, "Can I keep it?"

I whispered back, "If you keep it, how can you pay God what is due to HIM?"

With a joke in her mouth, she replied, "When I see HIM."

I giggled, and said, "Lyn when we get up front put that money in the basket."

"Ok" she spoke with a smile.

We followed the lady in front of us and walked towards the pulpit. I glanced at the pastor, and he nodded his head. We went back to our seats. The men prayed over the offering and went in the back. The pastor got up, and said, "Bow your heads."

Everyone did as commanded; even my little Lyn. I smiled at her obedience. The Man of God said loudly, "Lord open the ears of all within the sound of my voice. Let them get what the message has for them and let it feed their soul and guide them to YOU. I ask that YOU use me in a mighty way to bring forth YOUR Word as YOU call for me to do so. I ask it all in the mighty name of Jesus, Amen."

"Amen" everyone said.

The pastor looked up, and said, "James Crook once said, "the man who wants to lead the orchestra must first turn his back to the crowd." No one said as word as he said, "Let that sink in for a minute." He waited for a few more seconds to ask, "Who in here has felt alone? Let me see a show of hands."

I lightly raised my hand and so did a few others. He asked, "Now let me see a show of hands of those who has thought about giving up and letting it all go."

Again, I among others raised my hand. He said with a look of "I understand how you felt" as he said with remorse, "Sometimes we don't want to be a loner. We want to be wanted and needed. It's human nature, but what about God's nature? Sometimes, we don't want to be left out; therefore, we would rather hang with people who mean us no good. They are the ones who are the deadliest because we love them or trust them with our life. What about trusting God that much? What about trusting HIM with your life. Since HE did give you life? Your mom and dad could not give you life. HE used them to bring forth you so what about God, the man you have turned your back on? We want to have it all, but we can't. Not on this earth, anyway. When we turn our back on the world, we can face God. We in good conscious can't expect to face the crowd and still keep God. Your attention isn't that long, and God is a jealous God, for HE says to have no other God's before HIM and when you face the crowd you can't lead the orchestra. In other words, you can't face God and keep everything else. It is in your darkest hour when the enemy comes to attack you. This is the point in your life he wants you to feel abandoned so he can talk to you. He wants to be the still voice that tells you what to do and, in many cases, many will take heed to the lifeless possibilities he throws at you. But today I am here to tell you the Lord wants you to pour out of your soul the old you so HE can fill you with HIM to make a new you. The Lord wants you to go to your alter and pour out your significant other, your children, your job, your money, your clothes your car and your way of doing things. The Lord wants you to come to HIM like a hungry child in need of loving from its parents, Amen?"

"Amen" we all spoke.

"People there is hope to be refilled by Christ, but you can't be filled by HIM until you empty you out. You got to get out your own way. We all know who we are and can be our own worst enemy and that is because our flesh acts up and tells us one thing while Christ tries to tell us another. The problem is we don't want to pour out anything. We want to keep this and that and still think the Lord will fill us up. HE cannot fill up a picture with just one glass. HE doesn't want to add to you on top of other things that hinder you. HIS Word tells us old things are passed away and all things become new. Before the new can come, the old has to leave and you can't be filled with HIM until the old you get out the way, Amen?"

"Amen" I spoke, for I understood what he was saying.

The minister said, "You must get the mentality if someone is dead in God, meaning they don't have the love of God for God is love, but if they don't have God, they don't need to have you. They are already dead; you don't need them to take you to the grave. The old you is doing that for you. You need to be in the presence of people who believe that God is, God was, and God will be. God is Alpha and Omega, God was there all the time and God will be there all the time, especially in the right now situation." He moved from the podium to speak as if he was having a casual conversation with friends when he blunted out, "Ourselves will tell ourselves what we want. We don't realize that Our Lord Jesus will make man give unto your bosom. HE has blessings set up for you and it's up to you to get it. You can't expect to have or receive the blessings of God if you are you. HE can't use you in your present state. You can lead someone to the middle of nowhere, and then what? The Word says "They are blind men leading blind men. When a blind man leads a blind man, they both end up in the ditch." You don't need someone who doesn't know their way to help lead your way. All of this is where the Holy Spirit comes in to lead and guide you to all truths. Until then you are subject to about anything. Think about the widow woman in the bible. She had nothing and was advised to go to her neighbors. The Lord was making her a businesswoman to feed her family. If you have the Spirit of God, you can be led as to where to go and what to do because if you aren't led by the Spirit of God you are led by your flesh. One or the other is guiding you while you are in this earth."

The minister went back to the podium to say, "The most dangerous people in the world are the ones who do not realize they are wrong. They don't think what they are doing is wrong because of their motives. For that cause, the Lord HE created evil for that purpose. Evil happens so the Lord in many cases can choose to show HIMSELF strong to you. Things aren't always bad, they can be good, too. The enemy will have you holding on to dead people in dead situations just to keep you down. The enemy will have you thinking within yourself how that person isn't bad all the time or how they helped me so I can help them. You are being held captive without a gun. You are being a slave to people who mean you no good. The Lord says, **"HE will supply all your needs"** and if you have a want, seek HIM for HE will give you the desires of your heart. You see how all this depends on you? Can't you see all of this depends if you want to face the crowd or lead the orchestra. You can't do both. One of them will come up lacking and only you can decide which one it will be."

He put some things on my mind. I began to think, *who do I listen too? I quickly thought of my voices of reason. I listen to Tammy, now Henry and once Cedric. These people are the ones who mean something to me and for them I take heed; although Henry is new to me personally, I can tell it's gonna be more. However, Cedric has been on the back*

*burner because of his affair. Cedric has already hurt me,
and I don't want to endure another heart ache. His very
presence still does something to me after all these months. I
long for him to say, "babe I made a mistake," but I refuse to
play runner up to any woman on earth. I deserve to be just
as happy as my husband is. He has moved on and hasn't
given me or the girls a second thought.*

*When it comes to my new best bud Henry, he has his
own issues and being friends is the upmost important to us
both. Although, I admire the way he interacts with the girls
that is something their own dad has never done. I love the
way he makes them a priority when I talk to him about my
goals. I also love the way he calls my name because he says
it with passion. I deserve to be happy.*

*We act like kids, and we talk like best friends. I
saturate myself in his presence because he knows how a
woman should be treated and tend to. He doesn't believe in
love and that is fine. He and I are friends and hopefully a
woman will come along and change his mind state. I just
cannot mess things up, but sometimes I wish I could because
he listens to me, and he understands me. We are friends, but
according to Tammy, I can have them both and it all, but I
do not want it like that.*

*On the other hand, I want to listen to Tammy. She
was there for me when I needed help. She hasn't steered me*

wrong at this present time, but her hoe ways are on the
watch. I don't need anything else to jeopardize my heart or
my feelings for that matter, so playing with feelings is out the
question. I want to do wrong, but I just can't. Oddly enough I
have more than just me to think about. I have them.

When it comes to me, I want to have rough sex that
takes more than my breath away. I want to be carefree and
leave my morals out of the bedroom. I just cannot be like
that. I will not for that matter. I still believe I can be happy,
but how can I if in this world, I have only seen promiscuous
at its highest being played out by the very ones I listen to?
When I thought of that, I heard the preacher quote, "Sandra
Carey is quoted for saying, "Never mistake knowledge for
wisdom. One helps you make a living and the other helps
you make a life."

I was stunned for he opened the message up with a
quote and ending it with a quote. The pastor spoke more,
"Back in the hands of the Deacon."

He went to the back and the Deacon got up. I tuned
him out because this minister has placed some important
things on my mind. I saw everyone standing and I knew we
were about to be dismissed. I didn't even hear what he said
because my mind was still wrapped around the message.
Who would have thought by coming here I would have a
different viewpoint on what I need to do? I sure didn't.

Henry touched my arm, and I saw how Lyn was taken with him.

Witnessing their interaction placed a moment in my heart. We smiled at people as we walked to the car. Men tried stopping him, but he kept on going. He was acting like I was his wife, and we were his family. He saw me paying attention to his actions, so he said, "They won't mean you any good."

He already knew what I would ask. I like that. Henry locked Lyn down and I locked Rossi in her seat. We began to leave, as Lyn said, "Mommy, I hungry."

"It's mommy, I'm hungry," I replayed back to her, so she can hear it correctly.

"Mommy, I'm hungry," she said in her adorable voice.

"That's better."

Henry looked at me as he glanced to and from the road to Lyn, and said, "If you can tell me something the preacher said today, we will go anywhere you want to eat."

"Yay!" the duo yelled.

"No, you have to tell me something he said first."

Lyn tried scooting over to Rossi as if Rossi was going to tell her something. Lyn sat back on her boaster seat to say, "Give money to God."

Henry gave that smile when he said, "You are right."

"Yay!" the duo yelled even louder.

"Where you both want to go eat at?

Lyn looked over at Rossi and Rossi smiled with her daddy's smile. Lyn said, "Pizza."

"Pizza Hut it is."

The girls started having a conversation on their own. Henry said, "I should have asked the woman in charge if I could steal her and her family for a little while longer."

"Too late you already have the family's approval," I spoke with laughter.

Henry touched my hand and I felt the sparks. He lightly moved his hand as to tease me. He acts like he didn't know what he was doing, but I am not that naïve. I know when a man wants a woman and my friend wants me. I smiled at the thought of Henry wanting me. I stared out the window as he drove. I didn't say a word. I would see how it pans out.

We arrived at Pizza Hut and we went inside. Henry got us a table by the window. Lyn sat by Henry and Rossi sat in the wooden high chair at the end of the table, while I sat alone. The girls got a personal pan while Henry ordered us a salad and a medium cheese pizza. I was kind of nervous, but let I that past because I was out with a friend and my family. Henry and I didn't talk much because he was busy talking to the girls and making them laugh.

We were at restaurant for over an hour when I heard his voice and looked around. He stared in my face and I saw the devil himself. I didn't know what to do. He saw that I was with Henry and he shook his head yes and walked out of Pizza Hut in his uniform. Moments later, my cell started ringing. I already knew who it was. I got up, and said, "Excuse me. It's C-e-d-r-i-c."

"W. O. W." Henry said.

I answered the phone, and said, "Hold on a minute."

"Mommy I want to spell," Lyn said.

"Spell," Rossi said.

"We can spell words while mommy answers the phone" I heard Henry tell Lyn.

I walked outside, and said, "Yes."

"What the hell you doing with Henry?"

"Surely, not the same thing you were doing with his wife."

He laughed in a mad way when he said, "Don't fucking play with me. You my damn wife and I don't want you to talk to him. I don't want you to see him and I damn sure don't want him around my children."

"Who has the children?"

"You do."

"Who left them?"

"I did, but I…"

I stopped him in his tracks to asked, "If I have the children and I know what is best for them since you told me to think of it as a get out of jail free card. Use it."

"That was then, but not now."

"Nothing has changed. You're still not in their lives, so let someone who wants to be there, be there."

"I don't want Henry."

"Why? He used to be a good guy when you were friends with him or did it changed when you changed wives?"

"I don't want to discuss that shit. I done told you what I said."

"I have to go back inside and enjoy a man that is enjoying me and my family."

I hung up on him and went back inside to sit down. The girls were laughing at Henry. He acted like a big kid himself. It felt good to forget about my life as I watched them all have fun. Lyn leaned on Henry and gave him a hug. I knew she was becoming attached to him and I was not sure that was a good thing. He gave her a hug back, and Rossi said, "My hug."

Henry got up out his seat and gave her a hug in her high chair. I loved it. He acted like he was their father. He did the things Cedric should be doing, but I learned that all men don't make good dads. We laughed and ate a little more.

Rossi rubbed her eyes. I saw she was sleepy. I took out the baby wipes and cleaned her up. I handed one to Lyn, so she could wipe her mouth and hands.

Time had flown. We have been there for almost three hours and it didn't seem like it. We got up as Henry left a tip. Lyn grabbed his hand and he led her out the door after he paid for the food. He unlocked the doors and we locked the girls down. We drove off towards Tammy's as he gave me the smile that drenches the panties. I know he could fuck me like I need to, but I couldn't think about any of that until I settle things with Cedric. I said, "He doesn't want me to see y-o-u."

"He'll be ok. You're grown and we aren't doing anything wrong."

"I know that and you know that, but he doesn't know that."

Lowly he said, "I don't give a crap what he knows or don't know. If he is feeling like that he should be here with you all and not me."

"I feel the same way. I don't want to talk about him anymore. I don't want that name to ruin the rest of the evening."

"Your wish is my command."

We didn't say anymore about him. We arrived at Tammy's. I didn't see her car. Henry helped me take the children inside and to the room. I could feel the arousal tension building between him and me, but I know it is wrong. He left out and went downstairs. I followed behind him to show him out. He was being him and I love that about him. He was always cool and it is never a dull moment with him near me.

I wanted to offer him a seat, but I know if I ask him to stay we might be doing more than talking and we shouldn't be doing that. He made his way to the door and I went behind him to say, "Thank you for making today a great day for the girls."

"What about you? Was it a great day for you?"

"It was, but that went without saying."

"I didn't know. You became distant after your phone call with Cedric."

"I was. He kind of spoiled it for me, but when I saw the way Lyn was all on you it made me forget all about Cedric."

"She is a sweet girl and just needs her father's love and affection."

"I know. I think the same thing."

"Now Rossi is going to be a follower because she loves her sister."

"I know their bond is strong and I am thankful for that."

We got quiet as Henry spoke, "I enjoyed myself with you all today. I really did. I thank you for allowing me to be with you."

"Your welcome."

"Did you enjoy service today?"

"I did. He said some things and I received it."

"Glad you did. I hope you come back."

"I plan to."

He stood square in front of me. He looked down at me. I know he was about to kiss me, but the flashing of head lights broke up the gaze. I moved back and so did he. Tammy got out the truck with a margarita in one hand and her purse in the other. Henry asked, "You need some help, Tammy?"

She took a sip of her drink, and spoke casually, "You don't want to help me so you better keep talking to her because I own the game. I'm the coach, the Ref, and the player."

He kind of laughed it off, but I didn't think it was funny, but I played along with it by saying, "Girl, you crazy."

"Shid let me get a few more drinks in me and you'll see just how crazy I can get with dick in me."

CHAPTER 8

Tammy went on in the house. Henry looked at me, and spoke, "I better go."

"Ok, hit me up. Let me know you made it home."

"Alright."

I walked off because if I didn't the night air might make me do some things I may regret. I closed the door and went upstairs to change into a pajama top. I never sleep in underclothes and after thinking what I have been thinking I might need to let the pussy air out. Closing the door on my girls, I went downstairs and lay on the couch. Tammy saw me and came over to have a seat across from me. I was grinning as, she said, "Give me the 4.1.1. and don't leave anything out."

"Don't you want to finish unwinding first before we get to talking?"

"Girl, didn't you see this drink in my hand? I'm already unwinding. You just start talking."

"I had a great time with Henry at lunch."

"Wait I thought you were about to tell me about Cedric and the slap?"

"I'm going to get to it, but today I spent the day at church with Henry."

"Did you fuck afterwards? You had plenty of time. I know when the girls go to sleep they are sleep and I wasn't here so did you fuck him?" Tammy came out, and asked as if I was going to tell her. I replied back with a question, "Really Tammy?"

"Hell yeah. I forgot how fine his ass was and you already know him so why waste time. Shit you supposed to have been with him before you met Cedric tired ass, anyway. Hold that thought I need to fix another drink."

She went in the kitchen and came back out. I continued loudly, "We talk about how we were supposed to have met."

"Bypass that shit. I already know that."

In an almost dreamy state I laid back and closed my eyes. Tammy said, "Don't yo ass go to sleep. We haven't talked because I been gone. We have some catching up to do so wake yo ass up."

I opened my eyes and smiled. I turned my head and stated to my friend, "I am not about to go to sleep. I was gathering all the day's events to tell you."

"Oh, I was about to say."

I closed my eyes again, and began, "It was wonderful. He was a complete gentleman."

"Again, bypass all that and get to the mushy stuff."

"There isn't any mushy stuff. We discussed our soon to be ex's and talked about life. He made me smile and I can tell he and I have chemistry. We laughed and acted like no one else existed but us. I really like him and it's scary."

"How is liking a grown man scary?"

"It is. I can't really explain it, but it is. He understands me and I never got with Cedric."

"Keep going," Tammy spoke as she drunk more of her drink.

"We enjoyed each other's company and service on Sunday was nice."

"Continue."

I smiled as I stated shyly, "Anyway, Tammy, he is like every woman's dream and it makes me nervous to wake up. He wants a family and he has no children. He has money and he is very handsome. I mean Henry is a very great guy almost too good."

"And?"

"And what, Tammy?"

"You expect the perfect man. If so open the magazine and pick out your perfect mate. I guarantee he only exist in a book."

I laughed at Tammy and she was serious. I picked up the book and threw it at her. She held tightly to her drink as she kicked the magazine back at me. I stated, "I may be asking too much, but what's wrong with wanting happiness."

"Nothing if you can accept the flaws and the fact men are full of shit. You get that you will be all right."

"Not all men are. Many just make bad choices."

"Hell, almost all of them do. I can almost bet Henry isn't as perfect as you claim. I bet he has skeletons."

"You might be able to say it, but so far he hasn't shown me anything else. Besides we are friends."

"Now tell me about Cedric."

"How did he get in that day?"

"I came home on my lunch break and he dropped by. I told him he can wait while until you get back and he better not steal."

"What he say?"

"He said he doesn't steal and I told him I didn't think he would do you like he did, but he did."

"Cedric was thrown off guard, wasn't he?"

"Yeah. We talked for a little while more about nothing and I left."

She drunk some of her drink and turned the bottom up. "I'm all out."

"You stopped by the bar before you came home?"

"Shoot yeah, drinks half off from six to eight. I was running to the bar like a damn alcoholic."

"You are sounding like one."

"I know. I have become a damn dick sucking drunk, but from six to eight I substitute it for alcohol."

My eyes went wide open as she said the combination of words. The last part was too much for me. It is her business, but I was just stunned as, she said, "No shame in my game. Depends on the mood a man gets me in. If he gets me right, I'll give him good head and if you don't give head, girl you stupid."

"You and your head. Go right ahead."

"I see now that is why you had problems with Cedric."

I laughed at her, and said, "I can promise sex was not the problem."

"You might not have been holding your mouth right, Ange."

"Tammy, shut up" I spoke playfully.

"I'm serious. When you're doing the deed, you have to do it like you have not teeth. You don't want to scar it up then you can't fuck for the next few days. When you going up and down on the stalk, make sure your neck is flexible because your sore muscles will interfere in the pleasure you give. Shit, I love giving head to a nigga, so he will keep coming back if you do it right, But, if he is a weak bastard like Cedric is, you can blow his mind and take him for what he's worth."

"Oral sex is meant to be shared with your husband. That is a special event not to be treated like bribery if your man is being good. The Word tells you to not let your marriage bed be undefiled and when you hop in and out of bed what do you think you are doing?"

"Ask a man if it is defiled when he's shooting nut up your nose and down your throat."

I laughed because she is only looking at it through the eyes of a worldly woman. Trying to make her understand from my point of view would not work. I smiled, and said, "Tammy, you something serious."

"I know why you think any man I ever fooled off with will let me come back and fuck his world up. I treat them nice and I won't do anything they don't want me to."

"How about Andre daddy?"

She nearly choked. Tammy put her drink down, and called out, "Oh Hell Nawl!! I don't want the mother fucker near my pussy or my mouth. He has good dick, but his ass did me dirty and it took a while for me to get over it. He stills texts me to check on our son and every so often he texts about wanting some ass or head. I tell him no and hell fuck no." I was laughing when Tammy said, "Don't mention his damn name too loud. If you do he'll be calling and texting me. I don't have time for his shit. Been down the road with him and not going back."

"What about James?"

"He canned. I fired his ass last week."

"Why?"

"You didn't like him too well, Ange."

"No, I didn't, but still though. It has nothing to do with me, but what he do to make you get rid of him?"

"He got old. I told him just that I wanted something new. You know my attention span short as hell."

"Something new like what?"

"Girl, I had to get rid of him. He was talking about getting married and shit. I don't want to settle down, at least not yet. I like dick when I want it and from whomever I want it from. If I want to lick ass or get my ass licked, I don't have to explain to no damn body about the shit I do. When you got a man or a clingy man you have to shake his ass and lie. I don't have to lie about shit if I am a much right woman."

"You feeling good, aren't you?"

"I need to get fucked tonight. That's how good I am feeling."

"I don't know who going to do it in here" I spoke as she laughed with me."

"Let me go change. I'll be right back."

Tammy left and went to her room. I closed my eyes and began thinking about Henry. *I am clearly smitten with him, but I can't get too caught up. I am after all still married, but that would be a thing of the past the following Monday morning.* Seconds later, I heard Tammy say, "Wake your sleepy ass up."

I opened my eyes and saw Tammy. She walked to the kitchen. I actually took notice how she was almost naked. She had on a thin tee shirt with her nipples piercing through the shirt. You could tell she didn't have on panties and the shirt was a little too short. It was her house and I couldn't tell her how to dress. We were there alone. Moments later her doorbell rang. I got up. Tammy said, "You expecting someone?"

"No, you?"

"Nope."

I opened the door and it was Cedric. I looked down and saw he had liquor in his hand and his wedding band on. I stood there, and he asked, "Aren't you going to ask me to come in?"

"No. Didn't I tell you to call before you try to pop up over here?"

"I forgot the number and I wanted to see you. I want to tell you I will be able to pay more child support plus give you money for yourself."

"Ange let his dumb ass in."

Stepping to the side, Cedric came in and Tammy said, "I see you brought a gift. This must be to keep my mouth shut?"

He held up the liquor and she called out, "Pour me up some of that shit."

He poured her some on top of her old drink. I just stood there looking as he said, "Come on and grab a seat, Angela."

I sat down across from him while he sat on the end of the big couch by Tammy. She asked, "Why you here for real, Cedric? Can't you see my cuz don't want yo ass no mo."

"I can't see that, Tammy. I see a woman I hurt and I am regretting it," Cedric said as he kept his eyes on me.

He said all of the right things, but it was too late. I didn't say a word as I listened to him and Tammy talk. Cedric said, "Angela is a great woman and I want to make things right. That's if she will have me and we raise the children together."

"Yeah I am a great woman who is going through with her divorce."

"I don't know about that. You are still my wife and I don't have to sign if I don't want to."

"You don't have to sign. I'm still getting my divorce," I stated seriously.

"You want custody of Marilyn or not?"

142

I raised my eyebrow at him because Marilyn isn't mine. She was his before we got together and I was supposed to have adopted her with him when we got married. I hated we didn't get a chance to do it. Sweeter than sugar, I politely reminded him, "You forgot I am listed as parent with you and she is very much mine as she is yours. If you threaten me again about custody of my daughter I will kill you and anyone who gets in my way. Those girls are my life, my family and I love them dearly. I will not be threatened by you or anyone. Is that clear, Cedric?"

He stared at me. I didn't care if he was a cop. Cedric smiled his smile that used to melt my heart away, but it has ice towards him. Tammy said, "Loosen up, Ange. Let him speak. The bastard brought drinks."

"Tammy, he can speak all he wants. I don't have to hear it."

"You know I was just talking, Angela. Are you afraid I can make it good to you like I use to?" Cedric said because he saw how serious I was.

Nicely I stated, "That is my last worry. I don't need your dick to please me."

"Now ya talking my subject," Tammy said as she drunk some more liquor.

"Angela, you and I both know this dick is good?"

"Was good. The dick was good. Past tense and if you were the last man on earth and I had to choose between you and a goat…" I paused as I faced my palm towards me to waved my hand by saying, "I would say come here goat."

Tammy started laughing as she stated, "I can't tell that lie. I don't give a fresh damn if he ain't faithful if the dick is good and the tongue is better. I don't mind putting pussy in a face."

Cedric smiled at me over the top of the bottle at those words. I must say I do remember how good he made me feel, but tonight I was unbothered by it. Tammy spoke like her normal self when it comes to sex as she made it clear, "I love fucking and getting a nut off to start my day is the best way to start with a smile. We all grown and I know you know that I slang more than pussy than the average porn star. I love drinking nut while he plays in my ass. All this bitch between my legs don't get dick, this bitch in my mouth will make it up."

My soon to be ex-husband stated, "Is that right, Tammy? You like slanging pussy like that?"

"Hell yeah. Ange is a fucking square. Hur ass doesn't like to fuck and suck like me."

Tammy got up and began twerking. I didn't like the fact she was up and doing all of that in front of my husband, but I didn't say a word. I was over him and so far so good. I

144

glanced back at Cedric and he was like a man, enjoying the show as if I weren't there. When he saw, me looking he cut me a smile and continued to stare at me.

She finally got finished dancing and she sat down. She called out, "Turn the air up, Ange. It has gotten hot in here."

"Tammy, we both know you just started as a pharmacy tech," I said to laugh as I got up and put the air on 60 degrees.

Soon as I sat down, I looked at her. I didn't like the way she had gotten closer to Cedric. She got up and began dancing again and this time she was bending over and making her ass shake. He was still my husband and I do still love him. She stopped dancing and began drinking some more. Tammy asked, "Y'all want to watch a movie? Ya ain't talking about shit, Cedric and Ange this could loosen you up for fucking."

Cedric was already getting in the mood as I watched how he was acting and drinking. Tammy got up and put on a porn movie. Cedric kept staring at me. The movie wasn't doing anything to me, but Tammy was laughing and carrying on. On a few occasions, she would be talking at the TV and saying things like, girl, you ain't sucking that dick right, or I like the way he has his mouth all over her pussy and that is a good feeling right there to have someone put their fingers in your ass.

Feeling uncomfortable was an understatement as I tried to ignore her and her movie. She got a phone call and got up and went in the room. Cedric watched her walk off, and then stared back at me. He asked, "She feeling good ain't she?"

"That's her, but I'm about to go to bed so you can leave."

"You want me to help put you to bed?"

"I don't need your help in anything."

"You mean you don't want any of this" he spoke as he stood up cock ready.

Just by looking, it made me aware it has been a while since I had sex. It was odd I hadn't even thought about sex at all. I have been so focused on the girls and now Henry, that sex never occurred to me, even when I went out to the clubs. I decided to take a stand as I politely turned my head and looked away. Cedric came over to me, and said, "I am still your husband and you know I need you Angela. You hadn't had a man since I left over a year ago and you are still my wife and nobody gonna sex you, but me. I am your first and last lover."

How dare he throw up my lack of sex life to my face! I sounded really nice when I replied, "Like you needed all

146

those others before you got with Emma and while you were with me."

Cedric smiled, as he said, "That was the past. You forgave me and we moved on from that. Now let me move inside of that good pussy you have. It's wet isn't it?"

"Yeah, but you left me for Emma and that my friend is not the past. Regardless, how wet I am or not. You won't know."

Cedric stood in front of me, swaying his hips. I was feeling hot, but I remembered how unfaithful and caring he and his dick were to me. As nicely as I could I spoke loud enough to reach his ears, "Move out the way!"

The door bell rung and that was my excuse to get up. Cedric moved and sat back down. I went to the door and it was Jenna, Tammy's co-worker from the insurance place. She spoke and told me that Tammy was waiting on her. Cedric spoke, but he watched her walk off. I stood there watching him watch her. *A dog going to be a dog, even if it's a mutt* I thought as he focused back to me. I sat down, and he said, "I guess Tammy's about to get her pussy ate. You want me to do you? I don't mind licking your pretty pussy."

The nerve of Cedric made me shutter. He wants to take a special thing as oral sex to flaunt it around carelessly. I glared at him to say, "I think it's time for you to leave."

147

"Tammy didn't tell me I had to go. Hell, she done drunk up almost all of my liquor. I am not leaving quite yet. I'm feeling damn good and fucking you would be a great way to end this night."

"Suite yourself. Stay if you like. I am going to bed."

"May I go with you?" he said in a turn on voice that I know how good it's gonna be if I let him get it.

I got up and gave him a hell-no-stare.

"I can't understand that. I need to know if you need some of me tonight."

"Understand this, if you think I need dick, yo dick at that, bitch please. I can put my own fingers in my pussy and play with it. But, what I do need is for you to get the hell up out my face and out my life."

"No matter how bad I have been, I have never stopped loving you and forgiveness means a lot to you."

"I can forgive you over and have love for you way over there."

"You don't mean that."

"Why come I don't? You made me mean that. I'm at a point in my life that I can't let how you did me drive me with anger. I'm better than that and thought we were better than that."

He sat back and looked even sexier than ever as I went to bed. I don't even remember anything he might have said, but I do remember the feeling he had awaken between my legs.

CHAPTER 9

Soon as I went in my room, I striped off p, took a pm pill and went to sleep. No sooner than the third stage of sleep, I could see myself in the bed with Cedric. He had come in the room and began to undress in front of me. He came closer to me and picked me up. My arms were draped around his thick muscular neck. I laid my head on his massive chest and I brushed my lips against his skin.

The scent of his skeleton covering intoxicated me to a higher level. Cedric toted me over to the small one room balcony. He took his foot to further slide the door open and closed the sliding door with his foot before, laying me on the balcony floor. The moon was shining bright and the night seemed cooler, but as he came closer the coolness no longer mattered. The mood was right for fucking and the level of expectation was a record high.

At first I turned away because I thought about how those lips been on Emma. Each time he tried kissing me, I would turn away. When my husband looked down at me I felt like the only woman in his eyes. If he had another woman it was no longer important to me. We began kissing. His lips were as I remembered, inviting. It's been a long time since he has kissed me in this manner. He did a number on my senses as I arched my body to bring him closer to me. He had me longing for him. He pulled away from me and gave my breast the attention they deserved.

Soft moans escaped my lips for he was making my pussy purr. Cedric went a little further and my mouth fell open as he went all the way below my navel. One leg was thrown on the chair as the other one was prompt on the balcony. My husband hadn't tasted me in a long time and that night he did just that. I was squirting and wetting him up as I called out for him to stop. My hand began to tap out as my mouth called for more.

Before I could completely reach my peak, he got up and entered me with love. The wind began to blow with ease as we started to make love as if it was the last time. I removed my legs from their position and enclosed them around my husband. The words he softly heard was, "Yes, yes, keep it right there."

"Right there, baby?"

"Yes, yes."

Cedric picked up the speed and so did my body. I didn't care who could hear us outside as I threw my hips back to meet his. I was clawing him as his sweaty body was whispering to the depths of my being, "I love you, baby. I love you, baby. I love you, baby. I love you, baby. I love you, baby."

Our orgasms happened at the same time as he stayed on top of me, as his dick throbbed. He made sure to empty all of him in me and I made sure I caught everything he had. I could feel Cedric's arms trembling. He opened his eyes and stared at me with a look of relaxation. He smiled as his voice came back to normal by saying, "This was too damn good, Angela."

"I know," I spoke as if I just got back on the horse I fell off of. In other words, I found myself falling for him again when I promised not to.

He rolled off me and I went to the sleep. I got up the next morning from my bed with a smile and wet between the legs. *I must have had a wet dream* I thought, but when I turned over, I saw Cedric lying beside me. I caught myself for I almost shouted, for I didn't want to awake the girls. He had no cover on him and he was naked and hard. I acknowledged the fact that he still turns me on, but not like he used to. Carefully, I got up and shook him like I was trying to beat him. Cedric opened his eyes and spoke tenderly, "Hey, baby, you woke."

"Get the hell out of here!" I spoke through my teeth.

"This is the good morning I get after the way we fucked last night."

I nearly fainted as he got up and grabbed me. His body was pressed so close to mine that my nipples became erected. He sat me down on the bed. We stare at each other and I became lost. My husband leaned towards to kiss me and I almost gave in. Instead, I pulled further back to ask drunkenly, "Did I really sleep with you?"

He saw me being withdrawn from him and he pulled back to gaze into my eyes. We held that look for a moment as he used his hand to touch the valley between my breasts. I didn't know how to react to such manner. Cedric stated sexually, "Angela, it was that good that you can't recall the way I was going inside of you by making your body yearn for me?"

My first thought was *all the bodily fluids being transferred from him to me and from him to her.* I got angry and he knew it. I hit him with my fist as he said, "Calm down, Angela. I am your husband. I got drunk with Jenna and Tammy and couldn't drive home. I came up here to lay next to you. I awoke and pulled you in my arms."

I felt some relief; although, he didn't answer the question and if I know him, he won't. He'll let me assume whatever I want. I can remember the times he had made love to me and how I did long for him to take me and I also remember his sex being as good as a wet dream. Not knowing for sure I turned my head as he spoke, "Angela you felt so right in my arms. I can't lie I wanted you so bad and it was hard to control myself."

"I don't care how right I felt or what mistakes you have realized. You made your decision when you packed up and now I am making mine."

Cedric got up and stood in front of me. I said, "Leave before I get the girls up. I don't want them to see you here."

"They are my girls, too."

"Your girls have starved to death if they hadn't died in the fire."

"I'm about tired of you reminding me of that."

"I'll keep reminding you until I forget."

"That's not going to be anytime soon, is it Angela?"

He smiled, but his voice changed as he asked with an attitude, "When Henry started calling you?"

I froze as I spoke, "Why you want to know?"

"Doesn't he know you a married woman to a man that doesn't give a fuck about fucking his rich ass up?"

"Don't you know you a married man while you doing what you want, to who you want and when you want?"

"I see now I am going to have to pay him a visit."

"For what when you have his wife."

Cedric, put his clothes on, and spoke even softer, "Ex-wife. Come downstairs so we can talk."

"Give me a minute."

I put on my house robe and eased out the door. When I got to the bottom of the stairs I heard Cedric whispering in the kitchen. I distinctively heard him say, "I'm going to try and work things out."

I walked in the kitchen Jenna was sitting at the table and Tammy was standing in between them. They both had on a long shirt that barely covered anything and were barefoot. They all glanced at me and I played it off as I said, "Good morning."

"What is good about it?" Tammy said as she fixed her a drink to cure her hangover.

I sat down and Cedric went in the living room. My cousin said, "I see you had a good night." She sat at the table and closed her eyes.

"No. I woke up and he was in the bed with me. I didn't do anything to him. You guys got him drunk."

"He was drunk alright" Jenna spoke as Tammy hit her.

I didn't like how she used those words, but I asked, "What you mean?"

"He was just drunk," Jenna said as she changed her tone.

I glanced at Tammy and she shrugged her shoulders and placed her head on the table. I kept watching Jenna and she turned her head to look out the window. I got up and went in the living room where Cedric was. I stated, "I don't know what you did last night but you need to go before my girls get up."

"What you think I did last night?"

"I don't know. You tell me."

"Blow that shit out your ass. Why can't I be here to see my girls?"

"I don't want them to have the wrong impression of us."

"We are their parents and if they see us together there is nothing wrong with that."

"It is a lot wrong with that. We are not going back together and there isn't anything more to add to that."

"Angela, you are still my wife."

"Cedric, you are still my husband who left me for another woman so go back to her and stay away from me."

"I'll leave for now, but I am coming back."

Cedric got up and left out the door. Tammy came in as Jenna left out behind Cedric. I asked, "Why you bump her for? Was she about to tell me something about Cedric?"

"Not that I know of. I bump her for her to lower her voice. My head is killing me."

I didn't buy it, but I dismissed it. "Go back to bed and rest."

"I might just do that. I didn't rest at all. I got wore the fuck out."

I laughed at her as she went to her room. I went back upstairs were my girls were. They were sleeping and my cell phone rung. I picked it up and saw I had a few missed calls from Henry. A smile came across my face at the sight of his number. I clicked on it and called him back. He spoke, "Good morning, sunshine."

I glowed. No man has ever called me sunshine before and to hear it roll off his lips did a number to me. I could only reply, "I'm great this morning, but had a little rain last night and this morning."

"I have an umbrella to keep you dry, but tell me about this rain."

"Cedric came by taking outside his neck."

"About what?"

"About me and him going back together. At least trying to work it out. I told him no. He made his decision when he left and on Monday, I'm making mine. He then asked me why you calling me?"

"Why I'm calling you? What you tell him?"

"It's none of his business, and I told him nothing. He went on to say don't you know I'm married, and I told him don't you know you married? He said he's gonna have to pay you a visit."

Henry laughed as he proclaimed, "Let him come on."

"I know right. Enough about him. What you have going on today?"

"I thought I would take you and the girls to the park, out to lunch, and then out to the movies if you don't have any plans?"

He wants to spend the entire Saturday with me and the girls. I was polite when I stated to him, "If you don't mind spending your day with us, we won't mind spending our day with you."

"Great. I can come over and pick you all up around 11:30 or so. Will that be good enough time or you need more?"

"11:30 is perfect."

"See you then."

We hung up and I jumped up and down like a teenager. I woke the girls up. Lyn was acting strange this morning. I asked, "Baby, you, ok?"

"Daddy don't want us no mo."

"Why you say that, baby?"

Little Rossi called out just as serious as her sister, "No mo."

I glanced back at her, and Lyn said, "He not here."

"Not here" Rossi repeated.

I placed my attention on Lyn as I said, "Daddy is a busy man, and he will come see you soon. It doesn't mean he don't want you okay. He is just busy."

She looked up at me and gave me a hug. Rossi came over and gave me a hug. Those two has made my day and to know they need me to survive in this hoe world means so much. I waited until they removed themselves from the embrace before I moved. When they moved, I stated to my loves, "Lets' go downstairs. Mr. Darling is going to come pick us up."

Lyn made a funny face as she stretched her voice in a high pitch, "Mr. Darling!"

Rossi started laughing at the way she said his name and so did I. Lyn has always been the jokester even at a young age. After I found a way to stop laughing at her my words were, "He is nice and today he wants to spend the day with us."

"Ok" Lyn said.

Rossi repeated, "Ok."

"Ok. We have to get these beds made and our clothes on."

We made up our beds and I got the girls clothes out. Rossi wants to be independent like Lyn so I allowed her to put on her clothes. All she couldn't do, Lyn helped her. I loved the fact they help each other. I put on sandals, khaki

159

Capri's and an off the shoulder blouse to match. We went downstairs to eat some cereal. The girls went to their little table, and I put their breakfast in front of them. I went back through the living room to Tammy's room. Peeping in I saw she was slanted across the bed sleep. I eased her door back and went back to the kitchen. My stomach growled. I wasn't hungry, but I know I need to put something on my stomach.

Going over to the cabinet I fixed me a sandwich and a Coke. The girls had finished their cereal, and I cleaned up the kitchen. They continued to sit there until I tell them to get up. Soon as I finished, the door bell rung. When I went to the door, I didn't ask who it was. I opened it and saw Cedric. He smelled good and was dressed in his uniform. My husband had a hand full of flowers and from this point of view, sex on his mind. I was stunned. Before I could ask questions, Lyn saw him and called out, "Daddy! You not busy no mo!"

Both of them came running to him. He picked them up and gave them a hug and a kiss. *If only he could have been like this before all this happened,* I thought as I got a chance to say, "We are about to go. What you doing here?"

Cedric ignored me as he spoke, "These are for you."

He handed me the flowers without answering my question. I put the flowers in the kitchen and saw how I spent too much time picking out clothes for it was a little after eleven. Making my way back to the living room he had made himself at home. I asked again, "What you doing here? We about to go."

"Where you about to go? I come to spend time with my girls."

Looking at the girls I said, "Go in the kitchen and sit at the table while mommy talks to daddy for a minute."

"You gone leave daddy?" Lyn asked as if she were about to cry.

"Gone daddy?" Rossi repeated.

"No. I'm going to talk to mommy for a minute. I'll be right out here when you get finish, ok?"

"You promise?"

"Promise" Rossi repeated after Lyn.

"Daddy promise."

The girls left, and I asked, "Why didn't you call? I already told you not to pop up when you want. I am going on with my life and I don't need you cock blocking or thinking you can do as you please."

"Emma has left me and moved out of town."

"What does that have to do with me?"

"Her leaving made me realize how important my family is to me. I was just amazed by the things she does and the freedom I could have with her. I was thoughtless and inconsiderate of how you and the girls would feel. It took not having you for me to notice how I need you. Seeing you in this new light put a lot on my mind."

"And why are you telling me this again?"

"I am telling you how I see now. No more other people and that I decided to get counseling."

"Good for you."

"Why such short answers, when I am putting myself on the line for you?"

"You should have put yourself on the line when I was drawing the line. Now we don't have anything to talk about. I love you I cannot deny that, but you made up your mind not to have me or love me or do you not remember that day you smashed my heart?"

"I know it hurt Angela, but you can't hold me accountable forever."

"I can't hold you accountable for making me love you like I did but I can do something about what is happening now."

"Tell me you don't want to make this work for the girl's sake?"

"Don't you dare try to play the children's card! I don't want to make it work for them and especially for the sake of my heart. I can't."

I turned my back on him. He touched me and shocked me. He turned me around to face him. We both stared in the other's eyes as he said, "You felt that, Angela, like I did. Didn't you?"

I faced him and denied it by saying tenderly, "Felt what?"

He searched my face to see if I was lying and I was, but he didn't know it. He went on with his I want you back speech, "I still love you and I want to make it up to you and the girls. I know my actions were not one of a father, but it was my mistake. I want to date you all over again. I have to let you see how important you are to me. The other night you were right. I did take you for granted, but not anymore. I should have done all this when I had you, but I didn't."

"You did take me for granted and you waited a long time to come after me. To me that says a lot."

"Think about the girls and how they would feel to have their dad back in their lives."

"I am thinking about them and that is why I am pushing for the divorce. I can't have you doing what you like when you like then expect me to be waiting with my arms and legs open. I refuse to do that again."

I became solemn because I was hurt all over again. Just thinking about how he did me and how he made me feel caused grief to attack me. I continued to wait as he said, "I am willing to see you experience life a little more because of the things I have done, but you better not let another man fuck you and that I won't sit back and take."

"What choice you have when you left me? What you didn't think another man would want me?"

"It's not that."

"Then, what is it then? You were having all the fun you wanted and now it's my turn and you want to threaten me."

"I wasn't threatening you. I was merely making a promise, as your husband."

"Yeah you made other promises that you didn't keep like honoring me and loving me 'til death do us part."

"You always gonna throw that up in my face, aren't you?"

"That is not my intention, but I do want you to know and remember how you neglected your family away for free fucking when you wanted."

"It wasn't like that," he spoke with a little laughter.

"You say it wasn't, but you act like you didn't even hurt me."

"Hell, so what the hell ever! People get hurt all the damn time. They bounce back from shit and move on. So, what if I want you back after the shit I pulled."

"It doesn't even matter anymore. I am going on with my life and I suggest you continue to do the same."

Lyn came in, and asked, "Daddy can we come?"

He gave Lyn his attention as he called back to her in his delightful voice, "Yeah mommy and I finish talking for now."

I dried my eyes, and spoke with anger under my breath, "We're done talking."

CHAPTER 10

Cedric continued talking to the girls as I sat on the couch and decided to let him be a part of my past. My entire thoughts were of *Henry and the time I had spent with him. He and I would talk like old friends and flirt like missing lovers. I played a dangerous game of cat and mouse to a man that wants to catch me and hang me. I knew I had to make up mind about him being a friend or making him a lover. I couldn't have both because he couldn't have me completely because I was married. Taking on a lover wasn't the role I wanted to play. I believe in being monogamous in any relationship. So, having a lover part time or full time was out of the question.*

On a few occasions I have seen the way Tammy would watch him or make remarks when he comes over to see me or pick me and the girls up, but she crossed the line. I tried to keep him at bay, but it didn't work. I get where I want to see him and hear his voice. Sometimes, I could go to bed and imagine him making me stanking sweat from fucking me like I need to be. Again, I would get up and pray because I was a married woman and he was almost single with no ties.

He made me smile like a giggly girl who was unsure of her emotions. I could sit and replay everything he had said to me. I could even see the exact way he looked at me.

166

His voice got my attention and the way he lingers onto my every word did something to me. I try to talk with eye contact to assure him how he had my attention and to make sure I have his.

I didn't know how long I was in thought before I heard a knock at the door. I snapped out of my world to stop them, but the girls were already running to the door. I saw how Cedric was getting a little angry because his daughters were running to the door for another man. I smiled and tried not to let it show how I liked the way the girls dropped him like he did them. I turned to the girls to say, "Hold on and let me see who it is."

"It's him. I know it's him" Lyn said with joy.

"Him," Rossi repeated.

Fixing my clothes and being sweeter than ever. I opened the door with a huge smile and with nerves. It was Henry. He handed me some flowers and they were almost like the ones Cedric had brought me. I smiled and stated nicely as I could, "These are beautiful."

"Only the beautiful for the most beautiful."

"Where our flowers?" Lyn asked as she stood by.

I gave him the go head and he picked out two of my flowers and gave them to the girls. They were all happy and running back to Cedric to show him what they had. I could feel Cedric's eyes burning a hole in the back of my head as I stated to Henry, "Come on in."

He came in and saw Cedric. He nodded to my husband. My date looked at me to say, "I can come back if I am interrupting something."

"No Cedric dropped in for a minute and the time is up."

I looked over at him, and spoke nicely, "He was just leaving."

He got up and the girls were whining some as Henry said, "We can go another day. Let him spend time with the girls."

"No, you good. Isn't that right, Cedric?"

My husband did not say a word as he stared Henry up and down to say to him, "May I have a word with you outside before my family goes to the zoo with you?"

"I don't mind having a word outside, since the girls are tired of the circus."

"Ok be good," I spoke in a fair way.

The men went outside, and I scurried the girls to the bathroom. When they finished, I rushed out to the window, and they were still outside talking. From their posture, they looked to be friendly, but that can't be. Lyn touched my hand to say, "Can we go with my daddy?"

"Not today maybe later. Daddy has to go to work. Get your lunch bags and lets' go."

The girls got their bags, and we went out the door. When Cedric saw me and came over to me to say, "I love you, Angela."

As if he hadn't said a word, I walked past him, so Henry could help me lock them in. We drove off and Cedric was still standing by his patrol car, watching us drive off. Henry put on Kid Bops for the children. I was amazed he had that for them. I asked, "How you know they liked that?"

"I know children."

We were quiet a little longer as he spoke loud enough for me to hear, "You know he doesn't want me taking you out and spending time with his family."

"What did he say?"

"Basically, how he is going to win you back and be a better man and father."

"A little too late."

"Nothing is written in stone and if you want to give it another try, I won't be hurt."

"With all due respect, it's not about you."

"I know. I just want to make sure we are on the same page."

I smiled and he asked, "What?"

"I say the same thing about being on the same page."

He gave me that smile. I went on to say, "I plan to go on with my divorce. When I wanted him he played and waited until Emma threw him aside. Now he wants me to take him back and forget all the wrong things he has done. Henry leaving me was the first, but affair? It was not his first. I just kept taking him back because I love him, but now. No love like that again."

"You're giving up on love?"

"Never that. I still believe in love even if Cedric did me wrong."

"Ok just checking."

I smiled and stared out the window. My girls were singing and having fun as each song played through the speakers. I don't know what I was thinking, but Henry said silently, "We here."

As he pulled into this driveway, I saw how comfortable the place was. It was something about it. The place felt like a place I could call home. The neighbors are not close but are visual and I liked it. The house looked huge and peaceful. The girls stopped singing as he said, "We are here."

He and I got out and unlocked the girls. There weren't any no trespassing signs, so I thought *it was ok*. My girls started running in the huge yard, and then I saw a swing. I myself was amazed how big the yard was. The pictures on the internet do no justice for what I saw in person. Rossi, saw they swing and started swinging. I rushed over and told them to get off it because I don't know how safe it was and how I don't own it yet.

Lyn ran to the swing where Rossi was. I could hear Henry laughing because they were in full throttle to play. I had to stop and laugh because the girls were happy to run free in the country. There were people in the neighbor's yard as they waved over at us. I waved back with a smile. Henry said, "They like it. I can tell."

"I like it, but it looks expensive."

"This house has been on the market for a while."

"How do you know?"

"Look at the grass and it appears to not have life in it for a long time."

"Mommy, I want swing," Lyn yelled out as she looked disappointed to get off.

"Swing, mommy," Rossi repeated.

"Get down girls and come on."

"I can watch them because I see you have company coming."

They cried as the older people came over. It was a man and two women. They appeared to be about seventy or so. The younger looking woman spoke first, "Hello there."

"Hello. How are you all doing?"

"I am fine," she said as the others nodded.

"My name is Angela Hudson and the two youngsters on the swings are my daughters, Lyn and Rossi. The young man with them is a friend of the family, Mr. Darling."

They waved at Henry, and he waved back. I said, "I don't have a car and Mr. Darling agreed to show me this house."

"You like it?"

"It seems lovely. I would like to see the inside, but if it's as near as beautiful as the yard then I love it already."

"If you think this is wonderful wait until you see the house and the tree house out back."

A tree house? I thought how thrilled my girls would be to have their own little place. She smiled and stated, "We can go in and see it, but where are my manners? The name is Jewel Waters, and I own this house and acre of land. The other two is my sister Kimberly and brother in law Kyle. They are deaf."

"Oh. Tell them nice to meet them, too."

I saw how she signed, and they nodded their head as they left. Mrs. Waters said, "My husband Frank died five years ago and my children wants me to move up North with them. I don't want to sale it but I know they won't ever come back here to stay and neither will I. With that being said tell me about yourself."

I could tell the truth or a lie. I decided to be honest as I spoke, "Over a year ago my husband left me for another woman. I draw disability due to an accident before then I worked as a paralegal for The Hunt Brothers."

"They pretty good."

"Yes, they are, but after my accident I could have still worked, but I had the girls and no help in daycare for them."

"Shepard's is a good place if you stay around the way."

"They go there now, but I lived in the next town over in Lovely."

"Oh ok."

I began telling the truth, "The house my husband and I had burned and that caused me to come to my cousin's house about twenty minutes from here."

"You've been having it rough."

"I have, but it can only get better. It has to."

"It will, sugar."

We walked up to the front door, and she opened it. The moment I saw the large living room I was blown away. Mrs. Waters said, "This living room and the entire house were built by my husband. He was an architect and all he has done was build. I am a retired schoolteacher and when I stopped teaching, I worked with him. We personally designed it when our three children were about your girl's ages."

My mind was on how huge it looked. Mrs. Waters said, "The entire house is about two thousand square feet with a garage on the back along with a patio with a fire pit for romantic nights."

She bumped me and I laughed. She continued to show me the rest of the house, and it all was spectacular. It was a four-bedroomed, two-bathroom house with a nice kitchen and dining room. I could tell how she loved the house from the way she described everything to me. I stated verbally to her, "I can tell you love this house, and it means a lot to you."

"Oh, it does" she said with such a glow.

"Why depart from it? Clearly it was built with family and love in mind."

"It was. My children are all grown. My grandchildren and great grandchildren didn't spend a lot of time here, so they wouldn't know it means to live here. I want the person who buys this house cherish it like we did. I want the family to make memories and grow old here."

When she spoke those words my girls came in the house behind Henry. Mrs. Waters spoke to the girls, and Lyn said, "You nice."

Rossi repeated, "Nice." She smiled at Henry and Mrs. Waters formally introduced herself. She began showing us the entire house.

When she came to the three small rooms Lyn told Rossi, "This one your room near mine, ok?"

"Ok" Rossi repeated, and we all thought it was cute.

"This be our brother room, Rossi."

"Ok."

Mrs. Waters looked at me and smiled. I shook my head no. Henry didn't hear it as he asked, "What?"

"Nothing," I spoke as we both brushed it off.

Mrs. Waters made her way to the master bedroom, and I was in love. It had a huge garden tub and an extra-large shower. The color was calm, and the room had the atmosphere of love and happiness. Before I knew it, I said, "Wow. This is so freaking beautiful."

"It is isn't it?"

I amazed how the house flowed and when we made it to the kitchen and dining area I fell in love as, I said, "Yes it really is. I can tell you put a lot of time and love into this house."

"We wanted the best for our children because they deserved it."

"This house thus far has been well thought of and carefully planned."

"It was. I have enjoyed my life here, but it's time for me to move on to be near my great grands."

"Your home is really magnificent, Mrs. Waters. I mean every room has its own personality about it."

Henry added, "You can actually feel the difference."

"Thank you, Mr. Darling."

She walked off as Henry got the girls. He headed to the back of the house where the kitchen was. My mouth fell open as I glimpsed the glass windows all around so the sunlight could shine through. You could see a small pond and the entire back yard. When Lyn saw the tree house she screamed, "A TREEHOUSE! A TREEHOUSE!"

"Treehouse?" Rossi spoke as if to question her sister.

They took out running through the back door and onto the patio. Henry went behind them as Mrs. Waters stated, "The children love it."

"I love it, but I don't think I can afford it."

"There is no such price I could put on the memories here and the time I shared with my husband before his passing in the VA Hospital. I can tell you and the girls will do great here. I will make you an offer you cannot afford to say no to."

"I'm listening," I spoke with a little nervousness.

"Pay me five hundred dollars down and three hundred dollars a month for five years. That is eighteen thousand and five hundred dollars. What do you say?"

I could not believe a house like this at a price like that. Quite naturally I responded, "Why so cheap?"

"If someone wants to bless you, take it, and be thankful. Seeing you don't understand let me say this much. I am almost eighty and have no use for this house. I have a good feeling about you and if I can help a family I will." She made me cry. She gave me a hug, and said, "It's gonna be ok. Just don't forget to forgive as much as you can. My time on this here earth is not as long as you may have, but while I am here I want those girls happy."

"Thank you so much," I spoke, trying to hold back the tears.

"You're welcome. If you can get someone to mow the yard that will be fine. If not I will see what I can do. I will also have the papers ready in six weeks and when you pay me you can move in. Is that enough time for you to save the money or do you need more time?"

"That is enough time, but I don't know what to say?"

"Say yes and I will see you soon."

"Yes, and thank you so much, Mrs. Waters."

"Let me get back over here where my sister and brother in-law are. You can go out that way and I will lock the doors up."

"Thank you so much for giving me a break, Mrs. Waters" I repeated again.

"Take care of your children for me. This house is a wonderful place for them to have many fun memories with you and the one you love. I'm just glad you have a good vibe about you, honey."

I gave her a hug and left out the door. Parts of me wanted to cry because the lady didn't know me and she was willing to help me. Mrs. Waters waved bye to Henry and the girls as she went around to the front of the house. Henry saw my face and came over to me to ask, "What happened?"

"She is willing to sale the house to me next to nothing."

"What?"

"Yes. I have to pay her five hundred dollars down and three hundred a month for five years. It equals to eighteen five for all this."

"Didn't I tell you God is good and how HE is gonna have to come out the box to show HIMSELF to you."

"Henry, I am so glad."

"There's nothing impossible for God to do for them that believe."

"I believe it. I don't understand it, but I believe it."

"Let me tell you something. Jesus is not an unrighteous God that HE won't do things for us. Most of the time it is us who locks his hands, but not wanting HIM to do it because we want to do it or think we can do it."

"I can't wait until my faith grows like yours."

"Your faith can grow higher than mine, if you believe it can."

Henry gave me a hug, and Lyn came over to ask, "What's wrong, mommy?"

"Nothing is wrong."

Rossi came behind her and reached for Henry to pick her up. He did and we all walked back to the front of the house to Henry's car. Soon as I turned around and we made it to the car, we saw a police car. I knew it was Cedric. I don't even know how he knew where we were. I didn't tell anyone. He glared at Henry and Henry didn't show any sign of weakness as he continued holding Rossi.

We put them in the car and ignored Cedric as he drove off. Luckily the girls didn't see him and call out for him. Henry asked, "You ok?"

"Yes. I am. I am not letting him spoil my day with you."

"Mommy we hungry," Lyn said.

"How do you know Rossi hungry?"

179

Rossi said, "Hungry, mommy."

We laughed as Henry left out the driveway. He turned his attention back to the girls to ask, "What you want to eat?"

"I want chicken nuggets and a toy," Lyn exclaimed.

"Toy!" Rossi hollered out.

Then we heard Lyn tell Rossi, "Chicken nuggets and toy?"

"Chicken nuggets and toy. Nugget," Rossi said.

Lyn said, "We want to go to McDonald's. Can you take us Mr. Darling?"

"How about we go to McDonald's and on to the park?"

"Can we swing there?" Lyn asked.

"I don't see why not. Even mommy can swing" Henry added.

"I don't know about all that."

"Come on, Angela. Live a little. Your girls are only small for a little while. Let them see you smiling much as possible and demonstrating happiness."

I gave him a smile and said, "Ok. Mommy can swing, too."

"Yay!" Lyn called out as Rossi spoke, "Sing."

Henry caught the hint and turned Kid Bop's back on. The girls were singing and clapping along. That was a turn on for me. I thought *about sex.* He got along well with the children and they like him so far. I hadn't thought about their dad until I saw him and at that I wasn't thinking about him. Henry touched my hand to say, "I am so happy for you, Angela. You deserve it and I hope you do well."

"Thank you for taking time out to take me. If you hadn't brought me here today at this time, I may not have met Mrs. Waters and got the deal of a lifetime."

"It was all according to God's plan that's all."

We were holding hands as he drove us to McDonalds's. We turned in to the drive through and I saw Cedric's police car. Henry didn't see it. I was getting angry and feeling like he is stalking us. I pretended not to see him. He drove off. Henry asked, "You ok?"

"Yeah, I am fine. I saw C-e-d-r-i-c again following u-s."

"When?"

"A few minutes ago, when you were pulling in the drive through."

"Want me to talk to him?"

"No. Technically we are still his family and let's just hurry up and go."

"Ok."

When it came our turn to order he asked, "I know what the girls want. What do you want?"

"I don't see happiness on the menu, so I'll take a country style chicken sandwich combo with a coke for the drink."

He shook his head and said, "I'm going to have a double quarter pounder meal with a large coke."

The worker asked for his order and he gave her our orders and paid for them. I told my girls to wait until we get to the park, but they kept whining in hopes that Henry would give in. He looked at me and I knew he wanted to, but I made a stern face. We arrived at the park and it was halfway empty. We got out and Henry took out a tablecloth. He spread it on the bench right near some swings for us. The girls were about to dig in, but Henry said, "Let us bless our food first, and then we can eat, ok?"

"Ok," the girls said.

This was all new to me as he bowed his head and we all followed. He said, "Thank you Lord for this food we are about to eat. We ask you to bless it as it nourishes our bodies. In your name Jesus, Amen."

I said Amen and so did the girls. He gave us some Germ-X and we rub our hands together, and then started eating. The girls were quiet as they dipped their nuggets. Henry admired them and I could tell. He talked to them and they even talked back, especially Rossi. She was not repeating Lyn as much, but speaking more. He had fun with them and when we finished, he made the girls throw away their own things.

We all got up to go to the swings. He brushed up against me as he went over to give the girls a small push start. I felt an electric shock that almost took my breath away. I wanted to fall from the touch, but for some reason I didn't. I don't understand how being around him and having his slightest touch entices me. Henry glanced up at me and stared me up and down. I know he is thinking about sex because I was, too.

As if we were alone, I walked seductively over towards him to pick up Rossi and place her on my lap to swing. She and I began to swing lightly. Henry came behind me to whisper, "I saw how you were walking to me and it's a turn on."

Lightly he touched the drape of my neck and walked off. My breath became a little husky as my sense left me and chills showed up. *If he keeps this up, I might be tempting to fuck him.* Before the thought could process further, I saw Cedric. He gave me a stare in my face of one who was pissed as he sped off and turned on his lights, as if he had an emergency. Henry glanced up and immediately knew who it was. Thank God the girls didn't see him.

Henry came over to say, "You want me to have a word with him?"

"No. I can't let him control my life. He made Emma his choice and now tells me he and her and not together."

"I didn't know that."

"I didn't, either, but that's on him. I finally made up my mind to do what I have to do for me and the girls, and I can't have him trying to change it because his life didn't work out."

"Remember whatever choice you make, make sure it is one you can live with. I can tell you from personal experience how I have made decisions when I was promiscuous. I wish I had not done the things I have done, but I cannot change it."

"I understand what you are saying and trust me I have made my mind up."

"Mommy, I tired."

CHAPTER 11

We stopped our conversation and saw how Lyn leaned over the swing as if she could barely stay woke. Henry went over to her and brought the girls to me. I wiped their faces and hands off. The darkness had crept upon us and neither one of us paid attention to it. We enjoyed the company in our presence, but if Lyn had never mentioned about being tired, we probably would still be at the park.

He took Lyn from me and put her in the car. I had Rossi as she held onto my neck in a sleeping trance. We locked down and he drove back to Tammy's. The girls were completely unconscious. The night had gotten cooler and darker. He parked the car, and I got Rossi out as he got Lyn out. I opened the door, and Tammy was standing in the living room with a too small string bra and a pair of thongs on to match.

She just pissed me off and if I don't remain cool I will snap; her house or not. I had been noticing how she been dressing lately and I didn't like it then nor now. When we mention something about clothing, she would be quick to tell me how this is her house, and she can do what she wants. In essence, she is right, and I am homeless. I would play it off and change the subject as if nothing was ever said.

I'm just thankful the girls were still asleep as she turned around. When she saw us she kind of smiled and

185

walked back to her bedroom. I felt mad because my cousin, my best friend didn't try to cover herself up when she saw I had a man with me. This is the second time she has made it full known how she can dress when a man is here to see me. It's like she wants to show me up like I don't have a model's body like she does or how she can flaunt her sexuality loosely.

The first time she made it known was when Cedric was in my bed and now she's doing it in front of Henry. I know she has a well figured body and mine is thick and out of whack, but she shouldn't have to make it obvious of her intentions. She had the look of *I'm better* in her eyes and now I see my time here is like a snowball going downhill. When I looked over at Henry he had his head down; although, I knew he saw her. Silently I spoke, "Follow me."

He came behind me, toting Lyn as we made it to our room. He walked in and I used one hand to turn back the covers to lay Rossi down. He did as I did as he put Lyn on the other side. I watched him. He acted like they were his children as he covered them up with love. He faced me and smiled his adorable smile. I stated as I pointed to the sliding glass door, "Meet me on the balcony."

He went to the balcony as I changed and quickly freshened up into a two-piece pajama set. I opened the glass door and closed it. I stood by his side. He didn't turn as he spoke, "Tonight is a beautiful night to be spent with someone you care for."

"I agree. Are you thinking about Emma?"

"No I am thinking about you."

Henry moved closer to me to put his arms on my hips. He pulled me closer and stated affectionately as he stared into my face, and my eyes, "You are a well put together woman. I admire every inch of your face and your body. Your personality is beautiful, and your character is an original. I couldn't keep my eyes off you even if I wanted, too. Angela it's the plainness in you, which makes you simple but complex. Touching you like I am doing now, is something I wanted to do all day, but out of respect for the children and my conscious I kept my distance. It wasn't easy, but now they are asleep this feels so right to me."

I couldn't say a word as he smelled good with a hint of arousal about him. He didn't kiss me, but he pulled me so close and held me. I laid my head on his chest and inhaled his scent. He began rubbing on my back and I heard him moan lightly, which was a turn on for me. The man who held me affected me in such a way that he shouldn't. My was husband supposed to be the one making me yarn tonight, but he did not.

Our bodies began to sway as he and I went in a slow rotational circle. My hands were all over him. I had no idea how we got caught up. It may be the night air or the air of wanting the opposite sex, but we were. I took off my shirt and Henry stared at me. Henry made his presence known as he kissed me on the neck with ticklish kisses. He picked me up and I was astounded for he was nowhere near masculine as my husband, but he picked me up like I was weightless. He had my body's full attention. "Angela, I don't want to do anything you don't want me to."

"I am grown and so are you."

"We both can't deny the tension building up since the moment we laid eyes on each other in the park. You were so radiant and yet so alluring. How can a man not be attracted to you? Everything about you makes a boy scream and a man stay to see what the screaming is all about. You confuse me and still I can't help, but to hunger after you."

We kept staring at each other and Henry broke the gaze as he reached down and kissed me deeply with meaning. I loved it as I returned the affection. He stared at me to say, "I want to find out just how good you taste."

I stuttered when I replied with an edgy question, "You do?"

He made his massive tongue known as he said in such a way that my panties became soaked, drenched with wanting, "Why wouldn't I? I love to eat pussy, Angela? Yours smell vine ripe."

There was a pause as he said, "I don't want to know your flavor. I need to know your flavor."

"What you going to do when you taste the flavor?"

"Suck it all up. Then, I won't have to wonder how sweet your pussy really is."

I eased my pajama shorts down as he helped eased me out them. Henry lifted me up and sat me on the railing. He got on his knees, and said, "Hold on to the rails and keep your mouth closed if you can."

I held onto the rails while throwing my legs over his shoulder. He muzzled his head into pussy valley. I literally heard him inhaling my pussy with a long and deep sound. He lifted his head up, and said as I looked down into his eyes, "The inside of your pussy even smells sweet."

Henry made my breathing shake as he lowered his head and sucked on the left side of my vagina edges. He took his time to ease me into the oral sex play. I didn't know what to think, but to have him do that to me was not what I expect; however, I received the way he made me feel. My new friendly lover wasn't down there long for I moaned and rocked lightly on the rails. He made my breasts become rockets for they were taking off on their own. He knew how to eat pussy and not just that he gave me what my husband been giving away to another woman.

With that thought in mind, Henry eased off me. I thought he was finished. Out of nowhere he went back at it again. Making me crave his oral sex style. I was completely aware of the way his tongue went back and forth to the top of my vagina and peeped in and out the hidden hole. My voice of reason, my love was pleasing me as a woman should be pleased. *How could I have not let him do this to me earlier?* I thought. The way I felt made me not able to hold out much longer.

The heat of the moment caused me murmur out the words, "Let me suck your dick." I have no idea if he didn't hear me. I spoke it a lot louder, "Let me suck your dick."

He ignored me as he continued pleasing a pussy that was long in need of loving care. I was leaking so much that my ass was moist and in need of a jabbing. However, Henry didn't let up as I smashed his shoulders under my knees. I cried out like a person who just won the jackpot. It did not bother him about my sounds. This man never let his tongue let up with the wiggling he was doing. I in a way was exhausted and don't believe I could move another inch.

I have to stay focused and not go to sleep. The way he tongue fucked me, how can I not want to curl up and sleep for days? I hadn't had my pussy licked like that in a very long time. The awareness of having to feel him gave me the impression of needing some dick. My friend let me up as he got off his knees. I asked, "Don't you want your dick suck?"

"What man doesn't want a good dick sucking by a beautiful woman?"

Henry sat in the chair as I put the soft seating pillow under my knees. I kneeled down to see a huge dick with a curve. *Damn, I want to feel that curve in me* I thought as I touched him with my left hand. He lifted my head up to say, "Don't make me nut in your mouth. I want to put this thick nut in you."

I remember telling Cedric on our honeymoon how I wouldn't ever suck or drink another man's nut. Oddly, I felt obligated to remain faithful to that. I looked at the huge cock and thought, *Tammy did say he looks like he has a curve in his dick.* Pushing that behind me, I put my mouth on him slowly and from the small moon light I gazed up into his eyes. Pretending to speak into his microphone I removed my mouth off him some as my lips remained on the dick head. I replied as my tongue teased him, "I won't drank that nut because you have a curve I want to catch."

No warning prepared him for me easing my mouth onto him. He let out a rich moan as I took my time going from balls to head top none stop. Henry patted his foot as I took my time to suck dick the way Cedric taught me. My fellow acquaintance enjoyed himself as he pushed my head deeper onto his curvy stalk. It was unusual to have a dick of that greatness in my mouth, but it was a task I didn't mind taking on.

Because each time I came to his dick head, I had to slant my head another angle just to handle the wave. *This is truly a blessing,* I thought as I kept exercising his dick in my mouth. Henry was grunting and throwing the curve to me. Somehow, one way or another I caught the curve and swung back at him. He pushed my head all the way to the balls as he tried lifted himself up out the chair to meet my greedy mouth. He was no match.

He tapped my head, and spoke harsh, "Stop I feel my nut coming."

I ignored him like he did me earlier as I kept on taking him to the head. He tapped my head a little harder as he spoke as if he were out of breath, "I can't hold it longer."

I stopped and laid back. He raced out the chair to climb on top of me. I opened my legs in a one-hundred-and-eighty-degree angle to let him play ball. Henry stuck it in and seemed to have melted. He got himself together and instantly I felt the curve. He was hitting walls with it. Never have I been exposed to a man with a huge curve in his dick. I thought, *how in the hell did Emma handle it or left it was beyond me.* He knew how to throw strikes and high balls.

Henry from this point was a skilled lover. The man on top of me took full charge of me. I know now why he wanted some pussy. He wants me to feel the way he can make me moan and move. He was right. I loved the way he strutted his stuff in me. He had me keeping him at arms-length and I didn't understand it until now for the curve was dicking me down. This time I decided to work my pussy more at him to make his orgasm flow faster and it worked.

He sped up and was sticking me as if he were walking in a fast-paced race. I couldn't take it. I began having an orgasm again while pulling him deeper into me. His curve got stuck on one side of my vagina and stayed in that area when he called out, "Too damn good!"

I already had mine as I continued to hold him in place on top of me. He was right. The love making, we did was too awesome and I promise I want it again. Henry pulled his curve out of me. I felt it slide against my leg. He lay beside me to say, "I have had my share of pussy, but tonight loving you has been the best. I am not lying about that."

I replied, "It was good. I mean the dick was on point and you do eat pussy very well for an old man."

He laughed and so do I. He looked at me to say, "We crossed the line, hadn't we?"

"You don't think this constitutes crossing the line?"

"It does, but I don't want to lose you at all."

"What are you saying because you know I am still married?"

"I know what I am saying. I just hope you want to say the same thing."

"Which is?" I asked.

"Let us see where this takes us. I am into casual sex and fucking you is more than casual sex. It's like sex with a woman that will give the right man the world if he only acts right."

I smiled when I responded, "You're right. I will give it all to the right man, but I'm married to a man I don't know anymore. Not only that, you being a friend to me is more than what we have done tonight. I fear I have lost that in some sense."

"You haven't. I'm still the same person who will give you advice about what to do if you need me to."

"You can't give me unbiased advice if you fucking me on a regular basis."

He knew I was right, but came back with, "I know where my priorities are and so do you. When you need help or someone to talk to I'm still me. I'll still be there for you because I have grown to care about you and I know we not saying love, but something has taken place."

Before I could answer, I heard a knock at the door. I broke the embrace quickly by putting my pajamas back on. I went to the door and said, "Come in."

It was the hating ass Tammy. She said as she looked around the room, "What y'all doing up here?"

"We were on the balcony enjoying the light breeze."

"Won't y'all come on down and fuck with us."

"Ok."

That broke up the adventure as she left out the door. I went back to the balcony and said, "Tammy, wants us to come chill with her."

Henry was already up as he towered over me. I stared up at him. He touched my hand lightly and walked off. I had to force my legs to move. They literally became liquid from the moment we just shared. I washed off and changed into a short night gown with no panties or bra on before I could allow myself to come behind him. Gathering my senses, I saw him still waiting at the end of the stairs for me. He licked his lips at me and I swore my pussy said, 'Eat me, eat me.'

Next, I saw Tammy, and then I saw Jenna wearing nothing, but a string bikini over her light tanned skin. She has a model figure like Tammy and her own real long hair with blue eyes. Ever since that day, I don't like Jenna around me, but that wasn't my house, and she was not my company.

I stood beside him as he grabbed my hand and led me to the couch. I had hoped they would go in Tammy's room and do whatever they do, but they did not.

They both sat side by side, drinking dark whisky. Tammy started it first by putting on sexy music. I looked at Henry and he didn't say a word, but he didn't pay them any attention. Jenna got up and began dancing erotically as she drunk more liquor. Henry stood up and I followed. He said to me, "I think I need to go."

"Don't go, it's early" Tammy spoke as to woo him to stay.

He looked at me as I said, "He has to go to church in the morning."

"He can still stay for a few more minutes, can't you Henry? Do you drink?"

"I am an occasional drinker."

"Make this an occasion. Ange, you get you something to drink, too. I know it's been a minute since you drunk."

"Hell, don't y'all be a party pooper."

"What's it going to hurt?" Henry asked.

"I guess nothing."

Tammy got up and fixed me a huge glass of liquor. It had the colors of the rainbow, but she called it Hurricane because it's supposed to throw you. She gave Henry a large glass of rum and for extras she had alcohol Jell-O shots with gummy bears in small cups. Jenna asked, "Is it ok for me to dance again? I love this song, Tammy."

"Get your ass up and dance. I love to see you dance" Tammy spoke as Jenna got up wiggling and shaking her small ass.

Henry looked over at me and I didn't know if he was uncomfortable, but what man would be? A beautiful woman is half naked, drunk, and she's dancing like she is riding a horse. Tammy stared and threw dollars at Jenna as she danced seductively. A knock was at the door and Tammy got up to get it. I saw from the corner of my eye how Henry followed her ass. I felt hopeless when put up against those two. I silently removed my hand from his. He stared at me and I picked up the drink and guzzled it down quickly. He said, "Alright Angela. If you aren't a drinker, you will get drunk so fast. You don't need to get drunk not tonight."

The way he stressed, you don't need to get drunk caught my attention, but I was pissed at him for watching my cousin's ass. I roared out like a big girl, "I'll be ok. Thank you."

"What's wrong?"

"Nothing. You aren't my man so why should I act like you are?"

"Is this because I saw your cousin walk off?" He asked with those searchable eyes of his.

At first I said, "No." Then, I retracted it by saying, "Yes that's why."

"I'm a man, but I didn't mean to disrespect you. I just remembered when she was dating my cousin all those years ago. He used to tell us of the things she does when she is in bed with him and I thought about it when I saw her walk past me."

I didn't answer as I saw Cedric. He had on a muscle tee shirt that showed his newly ripped muscles. His hair cut was always neat and his teeth were always white. He was looking innocent and presentable. Even his Levi jeans fitted him in every spot. He nodded to Henry and said, "Hey, Angela."

"Hey Cedric. What brings you over here so late without calling?"

"I was off duty and I honestly hoped you wouldn't be asleep."

"What is it? You see I am awake."

"I just wanted to check on you and the girls."

"This late?"

He didn't answer as he said, "I see you are doing fine. Let me go."

"Don't go, Cedric. Have a few drinks with us. Ange, is even drinking some."

He gave me a stunned look of *what the hell* as he asked, "You drinking? What is the occasion?"

"I'm about to embark on my single woman hood again, but this time with children."

He didn't like it as he said, "Pour me a drink, Tammy."

"That's what I'm talking about. Get your drink on Officer Hudson. You might get lucky tonight," Tammy yelled as she jumped up and went in the kitchen. Cedric didn't watch her like Henry did. I noticed it, but he did look at Jenna as she was humping the air. He glanced back at me and sat beside me. He touching my leg was a turn on and I tried not to move so much for I didn't want to feel neither one of them. However, Cedric became loose as he drank. He was cordial to me and he acted like it didn't bother him to see Henry there.

Henry went to the bathroom as Tammy spoke to the crowd, "My mouth needs some dick in it. What can be done about it?"

I sobered up some as she said that. The only two men there with dicks was one I am married too and one I just fucked. Cedric laughed at her as she said, "Preferably if a man can't eat my pussy from the front and come out through my ass. He ain't Tammy ready. Ya hear me?" They all laughed, but I didn't. I pretended to be drunk as I heard, "Shit I will take a mother fucker out the game and bring his friend in. It doesn't make me any difference as long as they come to play ball or tag team me."

Cedric saw the look on my face and handed me a glass of liquor. He said to my heart, "Drink." I stared back at him, and he said with more emphasis and harder, "Angela, drink."

I took it from him and gulp it down quickly. I knew he was doing his best to keep me from snapping on my voice of reason. He was right to an extent, but I couldn't continue to keep quiet as she say what she wanted and get away with it. There was so much I wanted to express to that hoe ass bitch of a FAM, but it was not the time. Jenna said with a slur, "Tammy, you ain't ready for shit tonight. You and your pussy ain't ready for a damn thang, bitch."

Tammy spat at Jenna loudly as she opened her legs and thrust her ass in a rotation, "Like hell I am. Girl my pussy stays dick ready. What you talking about? You don't know shit about Tammy. None of y'all mother fuckers here know Tammy Janell Myers"

She stood up and almost fell as she concluded, "You got to be grown to fuck with me and if he don't have money he better have a damn good conversation because I'm about those damn Benjamin's. I don't give no fuck who I fuck to get what the fuck I want. Damn you and who the hell ever. Shid ya think I got this shit on my own? Hell mother fucking nawl. A dumb mother fucker fucked up and let me blew his mother fucking mind."

"Is, that right?" Henry asked as he came back from the bathroom.

"Oh, hell yeah. Ask yo cousin about Tammy, I'm sure he can vouch for me. Cuz, he knows I know how to break a nigga down. In case you didn't know let me tell ya. I own the game."

They all laughed, and I laughed some because Cedric had passed me drinks after drinks. Henry sat down by me and took a few Jell-O shots. I was feeling myself as I spoke up, "I been through so much damn shit that year that I've made up mind if anyone going to fuck me. I'm going fuck me. I'll buy my own toy and fuck my damn self. I don't need a real dick to buy me a toy dick to fuck." Tammy laughed as she said, "Hell, I play with toys all the time and I don't mind getting fucked by one as long as the dick has a curve. Shid the ones with a curve can go in you one way and pull all kinds of shit out as it goes back and forth. Hell, if yo ass weak, a curve dick can fuck your world up."

"What you know about a curve dick?" Jenna asked.

"I know too damn much about a curve that's what I know."

The only man with a curve I knew was Henry and I didn't know what she was implying. Cedric sensed me getting angry as I drunk to keep from fighting and being homeless again. If I am going for custody. I don't need to be homeless right now. I lay back on the couch and listened to Jenna cheering Tammy to put her foot in her mouth. Normally, I would have checked her, but a piece of me couldn't believe how someone I trusted so much could be so damn vindictive and cunning. Then again, I really don't know who she is talking about.

That night I drank like never before because drinking was never my specialty, but I would try this thing call living. About two hours later, I was up, laughing and dancing like I was in a strip club. Tammy encouraged me as the room was spinning around to me. When I sat down, I heard Henry laughing at me as he kept bumping me to stay focus. I heard him say, "Angela please don't pass out."

But I couldn't. I didn't know who said what, but I heard, "Let me eat it first. I know what I am talking about."

I felt my pussy becoming aware of pleasure as the mouth took a hold of my secret spot. *Henry and Cedric must been talking about eating me,* I thought as I wiggled to adjust my pussy. Not many knew how I like to be licked on and I don't know how it could be because my secret was being exposed. I tried opening my eyes, but they were heavy and the feeling was driving me insane with wanting more. Nothing I tried worked to see who was pleasing me; therefore, I relaxed and loosen up. When I did crack, my eyes open the lights were off. I was dizzy and it didn't matter.

My eyes closed back on their own as the wave of desire was taking control of my body. I could feel what felt like a tongue licking me and beautifully taking care of me. I know it had to be Henry because it felt all too familiar to me and too damn good to stop. The way my body responded to the mouth was a language it had spoken before. There was no way this had to be Cedric because of the flicking rhythm.

This journey I am on was made me rich with fever and wetter than water as I laid there and took the tongue lashing. I moaned louder as I heard slurping sounds in my ear. I know someone sucked on something and I didn't care who because I was getting fucked by a mouth. The secret lover buried their face between my legs and wiggled their head all around as my skeleton form started moving to their tempo.

I motioned my body to ride the tongue faster and harder like it was the greatest muscle I ever had. Truthfully, right now it was. The way this was going, I know he's not going to stop until I release the hidden liquid they seek. Because no one has tasted me quite like this and the way it was being done was taking my breath away and holding my soul at gun point. Another soft moan escaped my lips as I moved my hands to grab a hold of the head but instead I grabbed the couch.

The limbs I walk on were grabbed by my own hands. I had nothing, but pretty pussy in the air as they found the water spring. Slowly then faster I began to squirt all over the tongue and down the throat of my pleaser. My hands wouldn't let my feet go as I wanted the person to drink every part of me and they were. The dark lover was sucking on my pussy lips and gulping down the white sweetness from the pussy hole.

I couldn't stay there anymore as my legs felt like bricks to a newborn, but I managed. I couldn't keep holding them up because the lover wouldn't stop. They were being greedy with my body as if they hadn't had it in a while. I loved it as my body kept leaking out the good tasting nectar into the mouth of the hungry individual. Even when I felt like I couldn't continue to take the lean fucking I did. I kept a hold of my feet so the pussy would stay in the air.

This is truly being wild as the lover pushed me up higher and tongued fucked my ass. They were going in and out the anal as if it was as sweet and as wet as the pussy. I did without missing a beat felt my ass watering up. The way I was being overwhelmed by the mouth attack was phenomenal. With care, they tilted my ass back to the couch and began tasting me again. My pussy was truly up to it because over than what I experienced with Henry I was awesome.

That night my body was making up for the drought I had put it through. I wasn't even dry from the first orgasm as the mouth sucked on me with skill. I didn't know if I ever wanted to wake up from this display of affection my pussy was getting. I couldn't think of anything, but getting another nut out me. That time when I exploded, I damn near screamed from the joy I was having. Never in my wildest dreams have I had my pussy ate like that.

I let my hands let go of my feet as one fell on the side of the couch while the other stayed prompt up towards the back of the couch. I could still feel the enjoyment; although, it was over. My breathing was not returning to normal as fast as I hoped because of the roller coaster ride. However, my body was calm and tired. In my background, as before, I couldn't hear who said what, but I did hear, "You a greedy, bitch."

I tilted my eyes towards my pussy and swore I saw Tammy's face dripping wet with my secretions. She blew me a kiss and I went back out. The next morning, when I awoke still on the couch in the same position. My head was spinning as I saw Cedric on the other end of the couch naked and on hard. His hands were outstretched towards the other end. When my eyes followed his arms, I saw Jenna. Her legs were wide open and you could see her hair pussy covered with brown like hair. His hands were no doubt been playing in her pussy.

My emotions became pissed. I sat further up to gather my sense about what all has happened. My eyes didn't want to see what my mind saw about my husband. My head was throbbing as I stood to my feet. When I walked over to Cedric, I slapped his dick as hard as I could. He jumped up, but Jenna didn't move. She wiggled and stayed sleep. He got up and held his head. He took into account he was naked. When he looked over and saw Jenna above where his hands laid, he had a lost puppy look. He really had a guiltless look on his face as he saw what I was thinking.

It didn't look like he knew what had happened, but he was a cheater and a liar. What he has to say is suspect to me and I wanted to scream and cry. Cedric spoke silently as he came to me, "Angela, I didn't do anything. I promise. I would never jeopardize what I am trying to do, especially with a swinger like Jenna. I would not ever cause you more grief than I already have. You got to believe me."

I withheld my anger and my tears. My heart was heavy and I didn't want it to feel anything because he has already hurt me and I can't afford for him to do more damage to my heart than he already has. Taking my hands, I wiped my eyes to say with a crackled voice, "You don't have to explain anything to me. When tomorrow gets here you will be a free man soon to swing, which I had no idea that you did, but that's you."

"Angela, baby. I didn't touch her. Henry did."

When he said those words to my heart, I wanted to discredit him, but it felt off. What he said might have been of a truth, but it didn't feel like the entire truth. I spoke, "Why you want to lie? Is it because I am feeling him and divorcing you?"

"No. Angela, if you knew the complete truth about it all you would run and hate more than just me. What all happened last night is what usually goes on except you are usually not a part of it?"

"All of what that goes on?"

He looked around and said, "Nothing. Forget I said anything about anything."

"No answer me."

"You got drunk and were passed out long before things got totally out of hand, but I didn't touch Jenna. I don't even remember her being on the couch. Hell, I don't remember being on the couch."

Cedric gave me that sorrowful look as his mouth stated to my soul, "I love you, Angela. I just got caught up in the things of being free. I got my nose so far up Emma's ass, and the lifestyle that I forgot about what I was really losing. Please forgive me one day. I've realized how much being married to you means to me and plan to fight for you and for my family."

Cedric got his clothes, got dressed, and left. I wanted to be mad at him, but, how could I? He is married and this was the lifestyle he left me for. He kept saying how he didn't touch Jenna like that and he might not have, but the truth remains. I saw his hands extended towards her pussy. I looked around and didn't see Henry. I quickly went to Tammy's room. I opened the door and saw him in the bed with her.

They weren't doing anything, but it appeared something might have happened. I began to shake unquestionably as my thoughts went all over the place. She woke up at the top and saw me. I just stared at her. Henry woke up at the other end of the bed with his bare back showing. Tammy spoke, "Hey, girl."

208

As if nothing was wrong. Henry sat alongside of the bed as if he didn't see me. He asked, "How the hell did I get in here?"

Out loud I spoke, "I would like to know the same thing."

When he heard my voice, he turned to the sound. He appeared to be just as stunned as Cedric was about being caught with a woman. He glanced over at Tammy, and she said, "She talking to you. Shit I got drunk, fucked and fell the fuck out."

Tammy did not say anything more as she turned back over to go back to sleep. Henry got up. He was no doubt naked and on hard like Cedric. I do not know if it is from having to piss or on hard for wanting some head. I left out and he came behind me. He grabbed me, and said, "I got drunk."

"I've heard that line this morning already. Tell me another one."

"I did get drunk. Didn't you get drunk?"

"I did, but I didn't wake up in the bed with the hostess, either."

"No but you had," he cut it short.

"I had what?"

He stared at me in a blank stare. He smiled and shook his head to say, "We need to talk and talk now."

Feeling hurt and disappointed in another man I spoke lightly and coldly, "I don't want to talk to you. I don't care if I don't ever see you again."

"Angela, I am on your side. You got to believe me."

"The saddest part is I do in some form. I'm just tired of always being hurt by people I trust. Show yourself out."

I left him standing there and I heard him call out, "Fuck!"

It bothered me not. I kept on walking up the stairs. In ear shot Jenna spoke to Henry, "Let me give you a good morning fuck."

"Fuck you!" Henry screamed as he started walking towards the door.

"You've already did that, with your curvy good dick ass," she spoke in a teasing high pitch voice for me to hear.

I turned around and stared at him. He acted as if he was angry. She looked up at me to say, "What? If he did he did. Hell, he should have told the truth in this house of lies. I'm about to go my damn self because I can't get any rest here, too, much fucking and shit going on. Isn't that right, Henry?"

He got pissed and stormed out the door. Trusting myself to speak was out the question.

CHAPTER 12

The next 6 weeks flew by. I stayed out of Tammy's way and I have been avoiding everyone that ever meant anything in my life. I need clarity and keeping face with everyone was not the way to get it. I once heard if you want to see something you have never seen do something you have never done. I know I must get myself together and be about my business. It is not that easy for me; although, the advice Tammy had given me was on time it's just not my time. She hasn't said it, but I knew she thought I was hard headed and in a way unlearned.

After the newly discovered facts that the two men I want had the other two women in my face made me highly upset. I know I must kindle it. I have nowhere to go and no one to really to turn to. In a sense, I didn't know any more about who had my best interest at heart. It seems like everyone that comes to my path has something they either wanted from me or my heart. I couldn't afford to be in my feelings anymore.

Sometimes, I wished I could go back in time and redo everything, like I told Henry months before. I wanted my family back, but I can't ever have it back the way it was. If only Cedric hadn't fucked up and hurt me I would be happier. For me giving up and doing things differently was new to me. I have opened up more to Henry than I had ever

211

imagined. I decided to close my mind off everything and breathe. I been sneaking and drinking because I been in need of relaxation.

Since my encounter with them all. I stayed upstairs with the girls. I had Lyn get her and Rossi a snack and bring it back upstairs. She did. I lay across the bed all day and the girls were wondering what was wrong. I couldn't tell them I have a hangover so I played it off as if mommy was sick with a headache. They kept the noise down as they watched TV in the room. The entire time I laid on the bed I thought about the two men that has been in my life.

They each have something to offer me, but I don't know if I want anything from either one of them. My husband wants us to work it out. I can't because he left me for another woman. I refuse to be a part of that, although, the girls would benefit from having us together, but to what cost to my heart and mind? Cedric wants to prove to me how he is the man for me and I do want him to do that, but for some reason, I can't seem to forget the hurt and the part Tammy plays.

Just thinking about her name again caused my head to ache more. I reached up and touched my forehead. Lyn came over and touched my head as if she made it better. I sensed her compassion and gave her a smile. She got up and went back over to Rossi and began watching TV again. I continued thinking, *Henry is dear to me and has been in my ear for a while. The problem is we crossed the line. It was a line I wanted to cross at the time, but now I wish we hadn't. His friendship means a lot to me and he knows it. There is no way to undo what has been done, if it were possible to undo it I would.*

Because he is a kind man. I like him a lot, but he has hoe intentions. I can't be involved in fluently fucking anyone at any time. Life means more to me than getting my groove on or being a booty call. If Henry wanted more in life, which he says he does, but carelessly flaunting sex here and there is not the way to get it. He is divorced and he can do pretty much what he wants, but not with me. I am at a turning point as to not know who to trust.

My mind went back to Cedric. *He wants to show me he has changed and is worthy of my love again, while Henry wants to be my friend with benefits of course, but that can't be. I am a woman with small children. I will get attached and I don't need that, especially while still being married to another man. I shuttered at the idea of being with them both. I could, but I need to know where Henry's mind is at.*

I got up and eased to the balcony. I sat where I could see the girls as they were watching Dora on TV. I dialed Henry and he answered by saying, "I had been praying you called me, Angela. How are you?"

213

"I'm ok" I spoke dryly and slowly.

"I hope you can forgive me for being led by my dick and not my heart. Making love to you was the highlight of the night. I have never been with a woman before that made me feel like I was the only man she wanted. It meant a lot to me to have that feeling from you."

Totally avoiding him I stated in an uncaring manner, "I was calling you because I have a question."

He was thrown off and that is what I wanted. He replied slowly, "Ok. Let me have it."

"Cedric, wants to get back with me and wants me to stop the divorce. What do you think I should do?"

Henry was quiet as mouse. I know he is thinking. He said, "Do you want him back?"

"I do and I don't."

"Do you think you can trust him after all the hurt he has given you?"

"I don't know. I want him back for the sake of the children, but not sure about that, either. Parts of me want to go on with my life and be with you. I love the way you have time for us. You have been more of a family man than the man I married. You make me laugh, but being in the bed with Tammy is the drawback."

I know me saying that made me think if I even want to talk to him. This time he said, "I want you happy and I am not sure as to what to tell you. I mean I want you to be in my life because I have grown to care so much about you, but I do not want to hinder whatever it is you want to do."

"Do you think we can make a relationship and maybe marriage in the near future?"

He gave a short laugh as if he didn't want to tell me something. He went on to say, "I don't believe in love. I believe in making business agreements. To me people get married for that manner. It's not about a feeling of being with one person for a long time it's about what you can accomplish with someone to have more in the long run. If you have money, you naturally want to marry someone with money. You don't want to have all the money and they don't have it or don't try to get it. It's like this. If I made sandwiches on side the road and along came a woman with a store. I believe if we got together and I sold my sandwiches in her store, we could make a whole lot of money because of the business arrangement. Not only can people buy my sandwiches in a store, but they can get a soda or a bottle of water to go along with it. Do you understand what I am saying?"

"What if they are trying to get it, but not succeeding fast enough for you?"

"They can try, but after a while they must get it. If they don't you is the stiff holding the bag and the one who has to keep going in your pocket to take care someone who doesn't have the business sense like you may have. You don't want to be out of a hole, and someone puts you back in a hole you just got out of."

"Basically, you don't believe in love. You believe in business arrangements and profiting physically and not emotionally."

"Do you believe in love?"

"I do. I believe being in love with someone you don't want to be without. I believe in the funny feeling in your stomach when they come near or how they mention your name. I believe you are in love when all you want to do is be with them; even though, they have treated you like crap and you don't deserve the way they are doing you. I believe just the mere thought of them make you smile like a silly schoolgirl being near her crush. I believe you would do all you can to make it work and you won't stop until you give it your all. I believe you love in season and out."

He was speechless for a second before saying, "I believe you are a damn fool for believing in that. All you mentioned sounds good and fine, but love will get your ass hurt and your heart in your hand."

"You didn't love Emma?"

"I cared so much about her. I mean, what we had was good because we both knew what we were getting into. We both knew the lifestyle we wanted to live, but along the way I changed in some form. I wanted to settled down and have children. I wanted to be more than a stallion to many women. I desired to be a lover to one woman and that is when I met you and you have changed my view of marriage, but I know I need to come with it if I am to be the man in your life. If you are asking me if I could ever love you? The answer is no. I can provide for you emotionally, financially, and mentally and I can fulfill many of your wishes and needs. I can take care of you like a man should for a woman he is seeing. I can make sure you lack nothing. I can listen to you and teach you what you need to know if you are obedient enough to receive sound teaching, but I refuse to give a woman my heart. I refuse to trust a woman more than sixty percent because she is a woman and a woman can do all kinds of shit to get your mind fucked up. I've had it done to me when I was young and dumb. I've seen it done to the best of the best and I will not let that happen to me. If you ask me I will tell you. It doesn't mean you will like my answer, but at least you will know where I stand."

He has said so much and yet said nothing. I came back with the reply of, "That's because you never met a woman like me."

"If I had known you would be so sincere and caring I would have tried to find out more about you when we didn't meet that night. If I had known you would have been the one for me. I might would have tried more to find out where you lived, but if I had gone after you, Angela, you might not have the girls you have now. Your life would be different and so would have mine. We can only think about what might have happened but that is all we can do."

"I agree, but in a nut shell you are telling me that you will never allow yourself to love me or any woman because of your ideology of love and the human heart. Is that correct?"

"It is. I know you deserve the kind of love you are seeking, but I think it exist in a fairy tale. It's good if that is how you feel. I just don't and won't. I mean it is great to dream of the love you want, but to actually have it are two different things. If a woman or a man can find the love they seek my hats off to them, but not many ever do. Every day we are seeking or searching for another individual to complete us, but what about completing yourself and making yourself happy. Name one person you know of who has the ideal relationship or marriage?"

"I thought I did."

"What you think now?"

"I don't know that is why I am calling you. I wanted to know if you wanted to be with me the way I need you to. I needed to know if crossing the line with you was worth it.

We can't go back to where we once were after knowing where we have been. Maybe crossing the line with you was what I needed to see what I already knew."

He was earnest when he said, "Angela, pray you discover what it is you are seeking. I can tell you that I am the one for you, but I will not mislead you. I can tell you to go back to Cedric and that could be a grave mistake. I won't tell you what to do, but I will tell you this, I do care for you deeply, but I can't allow that to interfere with being someone you can talk to. I was your friend before the good benefits came along."

"You really think we can fuck the way we did, and no one gets in their feelings? You really think you can be honest to me on other men and not get any type of feelings for me at all?"

He laughed as he said, "Angela, the pussy good and the head is really nice, but I can't say that because I may fall into caring more for you and I don't want to do that until you are sure of yourself and what it is you want and need in your life. I didn't say us being friends has changed because to you I know it has. The way you fucked me and pulled on me told me, says you a woman who needs the love that only a husband can give and I am not that type of guy. Since my divorce, I don't want a marriage of any type. I just want to do me and do me when I want to do me."

"Do you want to fuck me now?" I asked trying to hide the anger because he was just in the bed with my other voice of reason and Jenna said he fucked her. I assumed while I was out drunk.

"Angela, just thinking about fucking you like we did makes my dick hard now. What does that tell you?"

"It tells me that our personal friendship is over and that we can only talk business. I'll call you back later."

I hung up before he could reply. I knew he was feeling me, but to know he wants to feel me and everyone else is a definitely no. A silent tear fell. Henry was someone I could rely on. I could call him or text him and he would respond. He has never been too busy to be there for me. When we talked we talked about everything. He was the type of friend that didn't come around too often and we fucked it up over for a very pleasurable night of sex.

I stood up and stared at the very sight where he had me up on the rails. I could remember the way his tongued pleased me like no other. It was the way he was taking his time to eat every drop of me, which had me wanting him to do it again. There was no way I could fuck off with him and still have a plain friendship. I knew it wouldn't happen and so did he. I assumed he was leaving it up to me to make up my mind if I want him and his good curvy dick in my life as a friend with benefits or nothing at all.

There was no going back to a platonic relationship after the way we got down last night. I sighed as Cedric came across my mind like clockwork. I walked to the door and checked on the girls they were still watching TV. I have so much going on and nothing was happening. I sighed and Tammy came in my thoughts. *Honestly, I could see her face wet from my pussy and smiling like she won an eating contest.*

I most importantly wanted to ask her about was she eating my pussy. My body tensed up and I wanted to feel sick. I would only participate in oral sex with a man I am involved with not a woman or my cousin, best friend, or voice of reason for that matter. I closed my eyes and my skin crawled. *The more I wanted to shake off the feeling the more it made me angry and wanted to confront her. How could she perform such an act on me and I wasn't a willing participant? Hopefully, I was wrong and it was a mistake. Something tells me it wasn't a mistake, but I have to ask her. I need to ask her for my mind's sake. What if she kicks you and your children out? What if she says she did it to you? What are you going to do? All kinds of things crossed my mind.*

I know I am going to ask her in due time. I looked up to the sky to say, "Lord I don't know what I will do or how I will react if I hear what she says. Help me if you never do anything else for me. It's more than just me. I have people in my life I don't know for sure about any of them. I ask you guide me in Jesus name, Amen."

I wiped my eyes for they were crying. I am so caring and loving and yet been done so wrong by those dear to me. My heart was heavy and my life seemed to be in a mess. I know where Henry stands now. I need to know where my soon to be ex-husband stands. I sat down at the table and called Cedric. He answered on the first ring by speaking, "So, good to hear from you."

"I hope it is good to hear from you."

"It can be. What does my wife need?"

"I need you to tell me the truth about how you feel."

"How I feel about what?"

"About me and the girls."

"You already know how I feel."

"I need you to tell me how you feel. I don't want to guess or go by what I thought because I thought we were doing good, but you have showed me that we were not. Again, I want you to tell me how you feel and don't lie. I don't think I can stomach another lie from you."

He was quiet as he said, "I have to go. I have a call coming in. We will talk later. I promise."

He hung up and I didn't like it. He always put others and his feelings ahead of me while I am the one always playing it cool. He only sees a reaction and not the action that caused me to act the way I did. About ten minutes later I saw Cedric's patrol car pull up. I knew it was odd and I didn't want to alarm the girls. I got my cell phone and I walked back in the room to say, "Stay right here mommy going to get some water."

I don't think they heard me and I was almost glad. I went to the front door and he did knock. I thought Tammy was in her room, but her door was open and she was gone. It looked like no one has been in her bed. He said, "Open up, Angela. I know you saw me pull up."

I opened the door and he pulled out his gun. I tried screaming but he said, "If you do I will kill myself."

He stood in the door to say, "I love you and I hate what I have done. I can't change it, but I love you with all my heart. I can't see myself without you. I been waiting on you to come around, but you been slow about it. I will continue to give you space, but I won't stop trying to get you back in my life. I didn't do right by you. I know I didn't. I lie not. No one here means you any good, but me and that is the truth."

There was no way I was going to debate with him about it. I wasn't going to say no you lying because he is the one holding the gun. I will not anger him or do anything to put me in danger. He gave me a hug and it was genuine. The way he touched me was heartfelt and filled me with so many emotions that it confused me. Cedric pulled away and gave me a kiss on the cheek. It freaked me out to see him so manly and yet so angry. He put his nine up and went back to his car. I closed and locked the door.

I was shaking and scared. My life flashed before my eyes and it wasn't about my life. It could have been, but it wasn't. There was no way I could hold all those emotions in that Cedric just gave me. As odd as it seems, I was not scared of him. I was afraid of what he could do. I just didn't know how to take what just happened.

Never in my day have I ever known Cedric to act irrational. He has always been cool and calm, but this evening he didn't seem like that at all. He was a different person and after what I just saw. I don't know if I want to be with him anymore, either.

My phone rung and it was Henry. I debated about telling him, but I couldn't. I answered the phone and the tone in my voice told him something was wrong. He kept at me until I broke down crying. Henry asked if he should come over and I told him not to because Cedric left. I needed to be alone. He said he understood and I was glad. It has been a long time since I have allowed my husband to get next to me. I didn't go to church because I didn't feel up to it. I just don't believe anyone understands what I am dealing with.

I love my husband, but he abandoned me and the girls. I can't let go of the pain he has caused me, but yet I still love him; although, it was not as strong as it used to be, but it was still there. For the rest of the day, I was in a daze. I was so glad my girls went to bed early. I needed to recap on the day's event. So, much has happened and in part. I understand how Cedric felt when he left me to do him.

CHAPTER 13

Monday came and I finally went to see the lawyer Henry told me about. The lawyer told me I could get custody of Rossi, but with Marilyn it would be a challenge because she legally wasn't mine. It broke my heart and being without my daughter would hurt me. I was crying as I called Henry. I have considered him as a voice of reason, but not the main voice I hear. He has been there for me and I know he is falling for me; however, he advised me to contact Cedric to see if we could work something out.

I called Cedric, but he was on a call. He called me back and I told him I want to talk to him. He was reluctant at first. He hung up on me and I felt hopeless. A few hours went by and he called me. I told him I want to talk to him and he said we will talk in person, but he won't be able to come by until a few days. I told him that would be fine. We hung up. When Tammy got home I told her about how I may lose Marilyn if Cedric doesn't agree to let me have her.

She decided to take the girls on a vacation to visit Andre for a week while I get some things together. I didn't want to agree, but I know the girls would love it. She told me she would not contact me unless it was an emergency and not to contact them. For I need to do what I need to do. When they left I felt empty and alone. The highlight of the first few hours was great. Tammy and I did text for brief moments to check on the girls. For the first day, I laid around and Henry called me asking, "Can I come over?"

"Why?"

"I want to see you. I want to talk to you."

"I'm sure you do" I spoke with attitude.

"Can I text you then, since you won't let me see you or verbally talk to you?"

"That will be fine. I must bathe, anyway. My head been hurting, and I have so much going on."

"How are the girls?"

"Being happy and being girls."

"That's good to hear."

I was trying to brush him off the phone. I was sure he caught the hint as he said, "Alright. I'll text only and see you when you let me. Hope your head feels better."

"Thank you. Henry, right now I need some me time."

"I fully understand."

I got off the phone with him and locked the door as I went to bathe. The water felt wonderful on my skin as I soaked and soaked. I got out the tub and dried off. I wrapped my short hair and put on my two-piece pajama set. It's nothing sexy, but if Henry takes it upon himself to come on over anyway he won't be surprised because he has seen it on me before. I went in the kitchen and got a Daiquiri. I downed it quickly. I threw the bottle away. *I must be thirsty* I thought as I got another one and another one. I poured them in a large picture and drunk out the picture.

These are good I said to myself, as I drunk more and more like an alcoholic. I heard music in my head as I began dancing as if I were on a stage. I got dizzy and fell. I giggled at myself for getting drunk with no one around to see me. I hope Henry didn't come because I was feeling myself and I hadn't felt so open like that in a long time.

The door bell rung and I knew he had decided to surprise me. I said out loud, "Oh, Henry, you're spoiling my fun." I knew it was Henry, but when I opened the door it was Cedric. My mouth fell open as I stared at him staring at me. I didn't know what to say. I hadn't seen him in a while and he looked handsome in all white.

My mouth, my lips, my voice box was all speechless as he asked, "May I come in?"

As soon as my voice could be heard, I spoke soberly, so he won't stay longer than he has to and he won't know I've been drinking, "You can stay for a few. I have company coming."

"I doubt you have company tonight."

I hate he stills know me, but I brushed it off by claiming, "Anyway. What do you want?" I spoke as I closed the door. He pulled from behind him a bouquet of flowers. I smelled them and they were fresh. I went over to couch and placed the flowers next to me as I sat down. Cedric said, "I want to play a few songs for you."

"Ok play your few songs and leave like a bad cold."

He took out his iPhone and I began to cry as I heard the song, *I'm Still In Love With You* by New Edition, my favorite guy group of all time. My husband, whom I never seen in that light before, did the moves that NE did as he sung to me. I could tell he put a lot of time and thought in this action. All the time he said I'm still in love with you or I'm still the man for you he would stare directly into my eyes; my face. He then said what can I do to right this wrong? Tears were all in my eyes and on my cheeks as he lip sync and performed the song to me to perfection.

When the song ended I heard On *Bended Knee* by Boyz II Men it made me cry harder for Cedric was in front of me holding my hands with one of his hands and wiping my tears with the other hand. The more he sung the more I involved I became in my feelings. He was doing something completely out of his character. Even when the guy was talking on the song, it was like he was saying it to me.

He said love can heal all things and how he is down on his knees begging me and he literally is. I reached up and touched his face. I don't know if it is the alcohol or me really feeling that way. Either way he had light tears gracefully flowing down his cheeks. Cedric was really doing something to me. When that song ended, our wedding song All of Me by John Legend played. I was at a loss for words. He was playing all the songs that ever meant anything to my marriage. He got up and I stood up with him.

Cedric held me close as the song played. I heard him whisper, "I never meant to hurt you My Angel. If you never believe anything else I tell you believe that I sincerely regret losing you."

I could not answer as I heard *Can You Stand the Rain?* By New Edition. I melted when he said what the guy said, "I know all the days won't be perfect."

My heart was saying yes, but my mind screamed no and to show him the door, but how could you when you are in the arms of the man you claim to love so damn much. All in my ear was Cedric's deep spellbinding voice and the musical sound of *Crazy* by K C and Jo Jo. I could only place my head on his chest as he held me closer to him with love. I looked up and Cedric said what the guy said, "I finally realize that you are my truly love."

To the end of time, I will not forget this moment he has placed upon me. The mood suddenly changed to a flashback of the times we had together. He went from *Twisted* by Keith Sweat to Smack That by Akon. Miraculously I was on my feet with him. We danced and having fun. I danced like I was back in the day with my ass all on him. I could feel him being aroused, but I didn't care. It was something he and I hadn't done since responsibility became a factor.

Cedric had his hands all over me and I loved being the center of his attention, always have. He touched me and had fucking a priority. I even caught myself singing to him. He and I were going back and forth singing and role playing. I didn't think he remembered the things we did but he did. At one point, I faced him. He pulled me close and allowed me to grind on him. He began kissing me in all the right places as I consent him to do so.

I lifted my arms and my pajama top came off exposing my nice breast. Cedric lean into me and began kissing them. I backed up and decided to make him come after it. I backed up and he licked his lips. Lifting my arms up to my shoulders and waved my body sexually and slowly. To look serious, I bit down on my lip, and closed my eyes. I began backing up towards the stairs. Almost immediately as my eyes were opened I saw Cedric coming towards me.

My pursuer was silently attacking me with his eyes as I looked helpless and guileless as to what is on his mind as well as mine. Upstairs my legs took me and Cedric came behind me. Soon as the door pop open he snatched me up and we landed on the bed. We were laughing as he said, "I do love you, Angela."

"I love you, too, Cedric."

My husband came closer and began kissing me more. All in my head, I could hear no, stop, and don't, but my pussy was screaming out oh, hell yeah, dick. I was in an one accord with my pussy as Cedric got up. I rose up on my elbows to take the sight of him. It has now been so many months since I had him. He was undressing for me like he did on our honeymoon. I easily took off my pajama shorts to expose my entire flesh to his eyes. He walked to the edge of the bed and began kissing my feet. Ever so softly, my toes one by one were in his moist mouth. I could feel the time he was putting into making me feel like the woman I have become.

Moving like we have all the time in the world, Cedric went up my legs as to tease my pussy with the idea that she may be getting tasted. Each time he came close to her he would turn away and go down the other leg. I was beginning to think he is just teasing. That time when he came up the thigh, he muzzled his nose into my hair pit to find the opening. Under a spell of their own, my legs did trepidation; for on their own without my say so began trembling for they know how satisfied his lovemaking can feel.

Cedric got on his knees and leaned forward toward me. The first few flicks of his tongue sent lighten streaks throughout my entire body. The more affectionately he tasted on me the more my toes wiggled and my lower half squirmed to his face. I discovered what Tammy been talking about. I really enjoyed the way he was sucking on my pussy lips with care. Cedric drove me wild. It must be the liquor. I was too damn turned on and horny. My husband made me want the dick more.

He did something with his tongue and I began to have an orgasm like an ocean breaking down the Great Wall of China. I clamped on his head with my legs and went wild on his tongue. Cedric was drinking me all up as I reaching up for the bed post and trying to claw myself out of a cave. However, my husband did not let me stop. He kept taking me for a ride I wouldn't forget as I felt my legs shaking and my voice strained.

Cedric got up with a wild look upon his face as he climbed on top of me. I couldn't help it. I opened my legs up wider as he entered me with a stout dick. I faintly hollered out "Cedric."

He started swerving on me. If he was churning butter, and then I was the bucket. My long lost lover made his body feed my hungry soul as he went in and out of me like a pro. I happened to open my eyes to see his closed. Cedric was actually making love to me with all he had and it is too damn good. This man I hadn't had in months has awaked a monster of an orgasm as I pulled him deeper into me.

Cedric kept moving on me as he was saying, "Ange!"

It seemed like he was running a race to the end, but with a strong tempo while the dick head thump inside of me. It was not like him to keep going as he nuts, but he was. Cedric was going on and on longer than usual. It blew my mind as he going deeper and deeper into me. With no warning, he became still with trembles and nerves. As if nothing happened, I let my legs fall to the side. Out of breath, I heard, "I don't want to get up off you, Angela."

He saying what he said made me smile some as he smiled. He appeared to be saddened as he started pulling out of me. I could feel him leaving out of me and I didn't want him to. Cedric laid beside me and held me tighter than ever. Calmly I snuggled closer into his arms and went to sleep. Wholly my thoughts went back to the long overdue moment I just shared with my husband. I know it wasn't wrong, but it felt right to be here with him.

For three days I didn't hear from Henry and Cedric came over every night when he got off from work. Me seeing him was reawakening my love for him. He and I would have fun and fuck all night until he had to go to work. He would text me like crazy and I would text him crazy. At night, he would wake up a freak and turn me out. He would have multiple orgasms each time we got it on. All he didn't put in me was drunken up by me.

234

Sometimes, it would be like a white-water form, and then salty. Sometimes, it would be thick and stringy as it drips from my mouth onto my breast. Cedric would video us like he used too and erase it. I hadn't tasted that much cum in a long time and I loved it. My husband was allowing his white seed to shoot up at me and when it slows I would finish draining it with power suction.

Cedric loved it. Each time we finish with sex, especially the oral he would tell me that he can't see me with another man. I would laugh at him because he knows I remember how he did leave me for another woman and didn't come see us. This night after we finished working out, I got up to air out the room by opening the door to the patio. I got back in bed and snuggled under him in my familiar spot. I thought *how I didn't want this to come to an end, but I know he and I must face reality.*

The girls crossed my mind and the thought of not having custody of Marilyn ache my heart, tremendously. I am the only mother she knows and Cedric doesn't even know where her real mom is and neither do I. Deciding to go back to sleep, my eyes closed, but not for long. He shifted some and mumbled, "Tam."

My eyes flew open. I answered nonverbally, "huh."

"Good head."

Tears wanted to form in my eyes, but I felt like my world collapse. I don't believe it. I couldn't believe it. I know if I say something the bastard won't let me get custody of Lyn. It took every ounce of love of her for me not to tear his heart out his chest and feed it to the dogs. He held me tighter. He asked in his sleep, "Why you tense, Angela?"

If I tell him the truth, I could ruin my chances so I did one of his numbers. I lied, "I felt cold that's all."

Cedric pulled me closer to him and continued to sleep. Without a sound, and unfeeling I laid there unparalleled to the fact of what is really going on between my husband and voice of reason? Almost immediately I got out the bed. My head was throbbing, but not like the pain in my chest from betrayal. Silly to think of such a thing and not know the entire truth, but I know something is not right.

When I made it downstairs to the living room my legs gave way. I fell down on my knees and cried at the end of the steps. I don't have factual facts, but I know something must be wrong because of this feeling deep in my gut. About thirty minutes past and I got up and walked over to the couch where my flowers were. I hadn't put them up since the first night he came. We been going to the fridge and staying in the bedroom fucking. I saw his cell phone. I picked it up and searched the contacts. I didn't see Tammy's name, but I did see her cell phone number in a text. I took a glance back over my shoulder to see if Cedric was up and he wasn't.

Going back to the hacking, I clicked on her text and read:

Cedric: gonna make it work with Angela like I said that day in the kitchen

Tammy: she don't want u she has Henry all in hur ass not u Cedric lol

Cedric: don't want 2 hear dat shit

Tammy: ☺ wat u want 2 hear???????

Cedric: shit from u

Tammy: ☹ wat u think Ange gonna believe, me or yo cheating azz?

Cedric: me I'll tell

Tammy: u won't tell shit

Cedric: I will

Tammy: tell hur shit or how ya like d fi head I give yo azz?

Cedric: fuk u dirty bitch

Tammy: no u d 1 fuk ☺!!!!!!!!

Cedric: wit friends like u who need enemies

Tammy: n wat does dat mean since we been FUKN b4 ya married hur

Cedric: ya call swinging fukn? Bitch plz

It wasn't enough to have had the feeling, but now I see the truth. My voice of reason, my best friend had at some point been fucking off with my husband. I threw the phone down and cried myself to sleep. This is too much for me to grasp. I live here until I can pay the money down and Cedric has the key for me to keep Lyn. Either way, I had to pretend I don't know anything for each has something I need.

When I opened my eyes, Cedric was smiling at me. I hope he does not think we are getting back together. I might have considered it, but not ever. I sat up, and he said, "I got worried when I woke up and you weren't there."

"I came downstairs for a drink of water and fell asleep on the couch. What time is it?" I asked to get his mind off me not staying in the bed with him.

"It's a little after four in the morning."

"Oh" I spoke as I sat up, making sure I don't touch him.

"Angela, you seem distant. You sure you ok?"

"I had wanted to talk to you about Lyn," I stated in a hurry to keep my cool.

"What about her?"

He had a blameless appeal about him and destroying his face is what I really wanted to do, but instead I stated, "I had seen a lawyer, and he said I may not get custody of Lyn because I never did adopt her with you." Cedric's facial expression became confused as he tilted his eyes at me. I sat up and said it again, "The divorce lawyer says I may not be able to get Lyn if you don't let me."

"I heard you," he said as he got up off his knees and sat on the opposite side of the room from me. I stared at him to read him. From this angle, he didn't look too happy to be discussing a divorce when he stated, "What I miss? We been making passionate love all week and today you talking about divorce and wanting Lyn."

"I had a weak moment for a man I love."

"A weak moment, that is all I was to you?"

"No, but for this week alone, yes. I was blown away by the memories you and I had created. When you came, and poured your heart into the dance and songs, I was recaptured, but I know you are only caught up in the moment of right now and not the- what is to happen, next."

"I was sincere when I came here. I caused my love to flow out my heart."

"When I was real, you played and now you expect me to believe you are want what you already had?"

He stared at me and for a moment, I thought I saw a tear. He dropped his head some and came up with the conclusion, "Is it Henry? Is he the fucker you want and that's why you're acting like this?"

"No, he was a voice of reason in my life. If you want the truth, you can't have one without the other. If you believe in love you believe in God because God is love. You cannot have love and say you have God. You'll be spirited and not spiritual. Henry doesn't believe in love, but says he believes in God; therefore, I can't have Henry because I believe in love."

Cedric was almost cold and cruel as he kept talking about Henry when he spoke, "I can tell he is after you and I don't buy that shit you saying, and him being just a voice of reason."

"I wasn't selling anything Cedric, but I was buying what you had until you said some things to me unconsciously," I spoke to make a statement.

He began to try and think of what he might have said involuntarily. I could tell he couldn't think what it might have been so he tried flipping it by stating, "I'm just trying to figure it out. I been open and honest with you about everything in my life and now you say us being together was just a plaything?"

"No, we are married and I wasn't playing anything with you. I know you have injured my heart and soul greatly. I mean if you want the truth take the time right now to tell me anything you haven't told me. Feel free to retract it right now or add to it anything you haven't said that I need to know so we can get it all out the open."

He was serious as he stared me over where I sat. He looked at my feet and stuttered some as he asked, "Didn't we reconcile?"

I would of thought it as being a dumb question, but we have been talking, fucking, and having fun. The best I had from him. However, I spoke calmly and sweetly, "But, there are some things I just can't overlook."

He knew as he asked, "Give me my phone."

I didn't move as he got up and got his phone. He saw the tear escape my eye as he opened his phone and saw it was on the text that he and Tammy had texted. He was about to sit next to me, but I lifted my hand for him to stop and he did. He went back to his seat and said, "Angela, it's not like what you read."

My shoulders went in a hump as the tears strolled down my face. I even saw from a distance how he had tears in his eyes. I seldom ever saw Cedric cry and here I am witnessing him doing it again. He stood up to put his hands on his hips to scream to me, "It hurts so damn much, girl! I made mistakes baby and I'm tired. For a long time I been crying over you and how I did you. Please let me explain and give me another chance. I won't mess it up. I promise I won't."

He sat down and held his head in his hand, as he cried very hard. I with tears in my eyes glanced up at him, and stated as clear as I could, "You don't know the pain I have felt about you hurting me like you have. I have vowed to not let you get this close to my heart and here I am in a moment of weakness, slip and made love to who I thought was the man that could still love me. It has taken me a long time to come to the knowledge of you not being in my life. I accepted it made up my mind to divorce and let go."

Cedric held his head up long enough to say, "Angela, I do love you. I was confused in the things I have done and the majority was before I met you. I want to start my life over with you and never ever bring this much pain to you again. Just believe me. I am the man for you" Cedric said as he cried.

Tears were all on him and wetting his chest. My husband was showing me a side of him I have never seen before. For the next hour, we both sob like babies fresh in the world. Whenever I thought we were finished we would cried more. Each time I wanted to say something to him, tears would overcome me and I couldn't say a thing to him. I also noticed how he would try to stop crying, but he couldn't, either.

A while later Cedric stopped before I did. He came closer to consult me and I let him hold me as I cried. He whispered, and said, "Let's talk about it. I will tell you everything concerning me."

He kept holding me and showing me the love I need as well as giving me the shoulder I needed to lean on. Before long, I sniffled, and said, "Ok."

He gave me his shirt to wipe my face. I stopped crying, and said, "Tell me about you and Tammy." Cedric looked away, and I said stern, "Don't deny it. I saw the text."

"I am not going to lie to you or make you deny what you saw. Do you really want to know about that?"

"I am in her home and she is fucking my husband. Sure, I want to know" I yelled at him to the top of my lungs.

He was deep in thought. He got up, and said, "I will only tell you about my part. You don't know your cousin, Angela. She is a bitch and a half. She is a devious one at that. She is like a dog eating its own young. As long as she eats she doesn't give a fuck who provides the meal."

My husband made a comparison like that was not like him. I stated, "I won't confront her or tell her we had this talk. I only ask when this conversation is over to give me my space and let Lyn stay with me. I am the only mother she has ever known, and Rossi and Lyn are in separable. I could not raise Rossi without Lyn, and you know it."

He was quiet for I didn't care about being his wife anymore. He left me for my dearest friend, and he has been fucking my voice of reason. He doesn't have anything to say I really want to hear, but for argument sake I will pretend to be a damn fool. Cedric shook his head yes, but his words were, "I will grant you all you ask, if you allow me to still love you and get to know you and my family all over again."

The love of my past life really wanted to make a go out of it, but not me. I came back with the statement, "We will see. I don't make promises like I used to with you."

"Anything is better than a no."

"What type of relationship you have with Tammy?"

"Without putting other's businesses out there I can say this. She is like Emma, but on a top-notch scale. When I say Boss Player, she is a Boss Player making some hell of a boss moves. Tammy will do whatsoever she wants. She is the type of woman that a man wants for a good time fuck. She will go with you and your wife if that is what you want. Hell, she will fuck the both of us if we both down like that. She doesn't have a heart the bitch as a tomato in its place."

"What does her lifestyle have to do with me and you?"

"I'm trying to let you see just who you call your best friend. She is the same one that will drink my nut while you at the store getting milk. She is scandalous and too far out there."

"Your point is?"

"I met Tammy through swinging. She and I use to swing together, but I saw you and fell in love."

"You used to date her?" I asked straightforwardly.

"Yes and no. I don't call swinging dating. It's called fucking who you want when you want. That is what she and I did for an exceedingly long time. Tammy is the fun time girl you want when you party."

"What do you call a very long time?"

"A year or two" I questioned with a surprise.

He saw my expression and asked, "You sure you want to know?"

"I do. I have to know Cedric."

"We fucked off for a year or two. It was straight fucking until her ass caught some damn feelings. It was too late. I didn't tell her I had met someone. I had to make sure the person I was going to stop swinging for was the one. And, you were worth it. I told her it was you and she was hurt. She cried, but I didn't love her. I cared so much about her. When she got over it she said she talked to you and she wants to back off because she knows how special you are to me and how smitten you are with me. We were friends with benefits that slept with other friends with benefits and with no strings attached."

"Jenna in on it, too, isn't she?"

"You already know the answers and I won't answer anything about anyone else, but me and what I know about

Tammy. You asked about my swinging with Tammy, and I am telling you that."

"You fuck her that night I dreamed of you and me?"

"No, I couldn't fuck Tammy, but she sucked my dick as Jenna ate her pussy."

I looked away and didn't want to hear anymore. Cedric said, "There is more, but I won't tell you because I don't want you to think I'm hating on anyone; although, I want to tell you. I will not let anyone else hurt you or use you. Is that clear?"

He has ripped my heart out my chest again. *How can the one you love hurt you over and over again? How do you stop the pain that grips you like no other?* Tears began to stroll over me as I tried saying, "I hear you and I hate you waited too late to play protector."

"I made mistakes and wish I could undo all the wrong I have done to you and the girls."

"Did we make love that night I woke up with you in my bed?"

"Yes, and it was so passionate that I couldn't believe that I had thrown such a faithful, and caring woman away."

I looked away again, and he spoke, "That night I realized how I would rather give up my life and the way I want to do things for you and my children. It was the way you made love to me."

"After you got your nut off you decided you wanted me?"

"No. When we finished swinging, I went upstairs and saw you sleeping. You asleep, looking so peaceful, reminded me of what I am in the process of losing. Here I am fucking and getting sucked left and right. There you are, the one woman that would do anything, but swing if I ask. Seeing you like that helped me to understand what I am losing. I know you think I am lying, but I made up my mind to let it go."

"What about Emma?"

"I told her I wanted my wife back months ago and she said she wasn't going to quit doing her. She left the next day and I haven't heard from her." I continued to be quiet. My love said, "Don't turn out like Tammy."

"And how is that?" I wanted to know.

"Don't be turning tricks and always searching for love and never finding it. She is miserable and wants to bring you along for the ride. Don't tell her you know about me and her. She will try to make your life hell. I know you don't believe me, but she is not the dear friend you think she is. It used to make me sick when I hear you call her your friend because I know the enemy she really is. Don't you know a lot of times when you and I were just dating she would try to tempt me to fuck her? Like that night I came over and she had on what she did. You in her house and what can you say about her in her shit? Nothing. Don't be blind to the fact how she is family. They are the ones who mostly hold the knife that cuts the shit out of you."

"I will receive what you are saying. I do thank you for being honest with me and telling me what you know hurts me."

"I know it hurts, and I didn't want to tell you."

"How did you know I was here alone and wouldn't be having company?"

"Tammy told me you were alone when I called her because you wouldn't pick up your phone to answer me. I thought something was wrong with you."

"I just turned my phone off and had planned to get drunk alone and get some sleep. Something, I hadn't done in a long time alone."

He kind of laughed as he said, "You're getting drunk actually worked in my favor."

Cedric is doing his best to read my reactions, but not today. I will not let him see how I am really feeling. It's my turn to play in the masquerade. He asked, "Where we go from here?"

"Right now. I need you to go, so I can be alone to digest it all. I do live in her house, and she does have my girls with her. She won't know for now."

"Ok. I have your cell. I want to call or text you to see if you all need anything. I will keep my distance from Tammy, but I won't leave you alone."

He got up and put his clothes on. I continued to sit there. It bothers me to even look at him, but I won't tell him. I will wait until I get custody of Lyn or however, I am faced with a bigger dilemma. A lying ass, friend, and bitch of a family member whom I trusted with my life. Cedric walked towards the door, and I wasn't sure I wanted to follow him. He paused in front of me to say, "Angela, you are the best thing that I have ever had and to know you are bitter in some way is a direction I never wanted to take you. As for Henry?"

"What about, Henry?"

Cedric stared at me in my face to emotionally bring out, "Keep your eyes open and your legs closed."

He walked off from me and locked the door behind him. I spoke loudly before I knew it, "Lord how could you allow me to be played in this way from my voice of reason of all people!" I did not hear an answer as I cried out to God. I knew if he didn't do something when I saw Tammy I would do something.

Pieces of me didn't care that I live in her house. She has been swinging with my husband, and she did it right under my nose. It would take every ounce of Jesus in me to stop me from whooping that ass when I see her.

CHAPTER 14

Tammy and the girls came back home the very next day. I was so happy to see my little loves and not too thrilled at all about seeing Tammy. I gave her a hug and spoke briefly to her as I became so involved in what the girls said. Talking to Tammy was the last option. I really didn't trust myself to be in her presence or even left alone with her. I knew I couldn't act funny, but it was human nature to frown upon someone who you thought you could trust.

I plan to avoid her at all costs, but on this night the girls went to bed early, and I became bored. The next morning, I thought she was in her room with Jenna or some young thugs like usual, but she wasn't. Tammy was on the couch, drinking, and being mellow. She finally caught me by surprise as she stopped me to ask, "Can you sit for a minute, Ange?"

"Sure, what's up?" I stated in a cheery way.

Point blank I heard, "Are you ignoring me on purpose or is it just me?"

That very moment was *the tell the truth or lie part*. I tried to be casual as I responded, "No. I have been focused on the divorce and the custody that I hadn't had time to sit down and talk to you."

251

She gulps down a drink to say, "I was finna say. I hadn't done anything to wrong you. Shid you FAM and I want to do what I can to help ya."

"I know you have helped me out in more ways than one and I thank you for going behind my back. I mean standing behind my back."

"Anytime, kin folk," she stated by drinking another swallow of her drink.

I knew she wouldn't get it, but I smiled, anyway. I continued to sit there. Over the course of all those years I'd been with Cedric I tried racking my brain to see if I had missed any signs of her and my husband, but there wasn't a clue. They hid their lifestyle from me very carefully and it hurts. Tammy asked, "You want to go out to the club week after next because the next two weeks I have to meet new people, if ya know what I mean?"

"No not really. The girls just got back, and I want to spend my time with them."

"That's cool, but shid you ain't chilled with me in a minute, either. Hell, you need to get out, get drunk, get fucked, and definitely get licked because ya know ya pussy can taste good because mine does."

Laughing I proclaimed, "What you mean by my pussy can taste good?"

252

"You a woman and women know what to eat or put on for a person to take it all off."

Doing my best to hide my fueling anger I spoke calmly, "Girl stop."

"I'm dead serious. You are going out with me and that is final. I will get a sitter for the girls and you just be ready for I am not taking no for an answer."

"Since you have made a decree about it, I guess I am going," I spoke to hide my displeasure.

Two weeks later and that Saturday came. I was glad it came for I had been counting down for the time I left the house. I had three more weeks, and I would be pushing on. They say you never know how someone is until you live with them and that was so true. I would never have imagined Tammy to be the way she is. Back in the day, she lived with me, and she wasn't like she was recently. The new Tammy is a bitch, and I was going to kick that ass. But, waiting on the perfect timing to confront her.

She did get a sitter for the girls. I got dressed up in a low-key fashion. I really wasn't in the mood for partying, but when you live in the house with someone you feel entitled to do as they ask even if you don't want to. It was almost like being a slave to someone or something. You know you live with them and if they ask you, in part you would do as they asked because your feelings will tell you how the person helped you when you needed it.

One day these feelings are going to die, I thought as I waited for Tammy to come out her room. *She came out the room half naked. She wore white stilettos, black laced see through pants, and top to match. You can see the white bra that didn't coverer her over size breast while I only had on a pair of black tights, heels, and an off the shoulder shirt. Truly she appeared to be on the prowl.* Disrupting my thoughts was Tammy's high pitch words, "You like?" as she did her famous Tammy-is-the- bitch spin.

"If you don't mind advertising the fun section of the toy isle, sure?"

She laughed at me. I never liked to show it all before a man could have it all. Tammy spoke casually, "This is how you advertise a good pussy bitch is on the scene."

I laughed my usual laugh. Tammy said, "Here."

She handed me an upper as she took two of them. I don't do pills, but I thought, *why the hell not?* I popped the pill and swallowed it. She said, "That is to relax us and get the party started."

We left out and got in Tammy's truck. I did feel a little weird, but nervous was the last thing I felt. The wind was a little cool, but right. She drove fast. We decided to get something to eat as time was getting late. It was about 11:30

when we made it to the club. Tammy parked her truck and threw me the keys, which means she was stoned and I couldn't get as stoned.

I went in behind her and the place was packed. I saw nothing but men. Fine ass men at that. Many appeared to be around twenty-one maybe twenty-three and that was pushing it. *A bunch of young ass men,* I thought as I scanned the place for men in their late twenties. None could be seen as we went to the bar. We grabbed a seat, and Tammy ordered us a shot of Tequila. She galloped hers down fast as she ordered another round for us.

Smiling in my face was a young man. He was sitting on the bend of the bar where he could see me. Men would come over and talk to us and Tammy being Tammy would embarrass the men by saying, "If you broke you can't fuck off with me" or "If you don't eat pussy, you can't get pussy."

Many of them would claim they have money, and Tammy would call them out. One by one would approach us and she would turn them down as she rolled her butt sexually on the table. She had all eyes on us, which faded me not. Tammy turned to me, and said, "You ok?"

"Yeah. I'm good. I'm just checking things out."

"You have to weed out the broke motherfuckers so the real motherfuckers come up. Shit time is money and money is time. If they have no money they have no time, you feel me on that shit?"

"Hell yeah."

"Shit I can struggle alone."

I'm In Love With A Stripper Remix came on and Tammy ran off to the middle of the floor. I saw the young man sit his drink down and come my way. I pretended not to see him, but his smell beat him to me. *Maybe mine hasn't kicked in*, I thought as I swayed my body a little to the music. He stood at the bar stool by me and ordered him a Remi on ice. His cologne was a turn on. I knew he was grown because you have to be twenty-one to enter. He smiled at me and asked, "Is this seat taken?"

"My friend was sitting there, but she on the floor."

I saw his wide pink tongue and my pussy was trying to take over the conversation. He looked, and said, "Oh, you here with Tongue Tammy."

He startled me. I glanced into his baby face. I guess the look on my face gave it away that I knew not the nickname. He kind of laughed it off by asking, "I'm sorry. What's your name?"

"That's more like it. My name is Angela. What's yours?"

"Darren."

I didn't say anything. I gave him a nod as he said, "I been watching you all night and I can tell you don't want to be here do you?"

"Not really, but I am here to have a good time."

"Are you?"

"It's ok."

"How can I improve the mood?" he asked me a question so innocently.

I smiled, and he said, "I should be more specific. How can I make your night even better?"

He is funny as I spoke, "So far I am enjoying the company you're giving."

"Just how old are you?"

"I look that young?"

"Yes."

"Would you believe me if I told you that I own this club?"

"No."

"I do."

"Really?"

"Yup."

"You don't look a day over twenty" I spoke with laughter.

"I am thirty-two."

"Let me see your license."

He pulled them out and I could not believe it. He looked so young. He asked, "You believe me now?"

"Not really" I spoke as I drunk some more.

"Even after seeing the proof?"

"Yes. It could be falsified," I blamer out with humor.

He laughed, and asked, "You want to dance?"

"No. I don't make it my business to dance with men because they could have a woman in here."

"No woman. Just me."

"It's just you, huh?"

He nodded. I checked his body over and could tell he was some type of athlete. His chest has the type of dent that made you want to place your head in it. His small waist spoke of a big dick. I got excited about a big dick. He asked with a sincere tone this time, "May I have this dance with you, Angela?"

My brain yelled no but my body screamed yes. Listening to the flesh I said, "Yes."

He reached for my hand like a gentleman. Soon as I stood, I saw Henry. He was talking to Tammy. He saw me and I showed my dislike. He came over as we began walking to the floor. Henry asked, "May I have a word with you?"

"I am about to dance."

"Fuck that young nigga. I don't care if he owns the place."

The guy was a gentleman, and said, "You going to dance with me or talk to him, Angela."

Darren stood his ground as my pussy literally leaped in his hands. I smiled, and said, "Let's go. I can't hear in here."

I left Henry staring after me. He asked, "Who was he?"

"He was a friend who wants to have benefits."

"Oh. What you want to do?"

My body said fuck as I heard R. Kelly's *Your Body Calling* in the blaring over the speakers. Thinking with pussy I spoke, "Lets' go somewhere so you can fuck the shit out of me."

This man smiled as he led me upstairs to the private room. He closed the door, and it was a room with a private bar and king size bed. To the right was a bathroom. I spoke, "You bring many women up here?"

"No, but there is something about you Angela, I like."

"What?"

He walked up to me, and I stared up into his eyes. He asked with a surprise, "You don't do one night stands. I can tell."

"I can tell that you aren't fucking me right now."

He smiled, and said, "I don't eat pussy on the first night and since you doing something out of character, so will I."

My legs became liquid at those words. I walked backwards and took off my shoes. Bit by bit I began to undress and so did he. I lay back on the bed with my legs closed. He eased by my feet and nibbled at the toes then to the arch. *Is he trying to make love of fuck?* I thought as he took his time. When he got between my legs they magically opened and waited for him. Darren used his right hand to open my pussy up from the top.

Fully exposed and ready. Half a second later a warm moist mouth found my pussy. He was gentle as he licked here and there. It wasn't anywhere near the tongue, whipping I got two weeks or close to the one Henry's mouth put on me, but it was nice. He took his time to taste me. I closed my eyes and enjoyed the oral sex play. I had a quick orgasm. No man has ever made me cum so quickly.

When I opened my eyes, the door opened, and it was the other guy with him. He was a lot taller, and I didn't know what to think until Darren said, "This is Coby. He's a friend of mine and we both want to fuck you. Would that be a problem?"

I have never had a train ran on me before, but thought *if I don't fuck my way out of here, I might have to fight my way out of here and from the looks of them, I would lose.* I smiled and said, "Which dick I'm sucking first?"

His friend pulled off his clothes and his dick was hung like nothing I have ever seen. I lay back as Darren began to feast on me like a starving Ethiopian in search of a good meal. His friend lay cross ways and sucked on my breast. I loved the way his tongue was rough and demanding. He heard me moan and got up to straddle me over my breast. He put a knee on each side of my body, and I had nothing but dick in my face.

The head alone was huge and round. *There is no way I can fit all that in my mouth,* I spoke to myself as I moved my head up to taste the dick head. Once I did that, that bitch in me woke up and began to show out. His dick head thump me in the top of my chest area as I used my neck muscles to work that dick towards my mouth. Once I got it at my lips. The rest was downhill as he slid it in my mouth.

I was sucking like he was a name brand sucker. He grabbed the headboard and began shooting his cock in and out my mouth and I was taking it like a real bitch take dick, to the head. The guy fucking my mouth was grunting and carrying on. I didn't realize how or when Darren lifted my legs up, and placed himself under me to enter me. *I hope he has on a condom, but I'm sucking dick raw* I thought.

The bed shook in every angle from their different rhythms. All I had to do was lay there and enjoy the ride. I didn't mind. It was new to me, and I liked fucking and sucking at the same damn time. However, when Coby began to nut, I felt his dick swell in my mouth, and I didn't want to drink his nut. I was no position to refuse because my arms were under his thighs. I did remember what I told Cedric about not drinking another man's nut.

Then, my mind told me how he probably done drank Emma and who else ever pussy liquid. That made my suction pull harder and harder. Coby tried to move back, but my mouth had a hold on his dick where he couldn't do anything, but cum in my mouth. His man fluid was bitter, but a lot. I almost choked as I stared up at him staring down at me. I sucked it slowly as if I were in love. He stared in my eyes and shuttered the remainder of his seed.

When he finished, he continued to have his dick in my mouth. I could not say a word, but I did still suck him slower until he found the strength to take it out my mouth. I licked my lips to get the rest of him on my tongue. Coby continued to stare at me and me at him. In a slow drag his dick made a wet slimy trail through my breast as he fell over to my right. He pumped his fist in the air many times as he screams out, "Darren! This bitch is good. Her head is on fucking fire."

Darren laughed as I sat up some, and said, "Next."

I saw the condom and felt a little better. Eagerly and in a hurry, Darren lay beside me as I faced Coby. He was still looking amazed at what I just did to him because I could see it on his face. Darren snatched me and slid his ok size dick in my pussy. *He's going to be an easy fuck. He likes the spoon style,* I thought as he shook the bed with his dick clinging in me. I wasn't fazed about him taking the pussy I wanted Coby's dick in me. Coby saw me and I reached over and put my hand on his dick. I began shaking it with each pump Darren gave me.

His dick began to rise the way I liked. Darren cum all over my ass cheeks and lower back. That's how involved I was into Coby. He moved out the way to say, "I wasn't putting this rich nut in you."

Being a full-blown hoe bitch that was caught in the moment, I spoke, "You should have put it on my face if it's that rich."

"I will. Let me watch Coby bust your pussy open with his mule head dick."

"Yeah. I need to see if the pussy is as hot as the head I just got," Coby said as he smiled at me.

Showing no emotions, I spoke as if I knew how to take a big dick, "If he ducks not good, please pass. No disappointments tonight."

I looked over and Coby's dick rose higher. He has slid a condom on and *I might are to shut the hell up,* I thought as I heard him say with a little attitude, "Get up."

I was kind of nervous as I got up. He picked me up and put me up against the wall. He smiled at me, and then I felt the powerful entry. His dick got strength as I took all of it in me. He didn't give me time to adjust to it as he suspended me in the air. This man was man handling me as he fucked me like a five-dollar hoe.

He had no feelings as he pushed his dick in and out of me. I didn't think he was able, but he held me up and kept smashing me on him. He was showing my pussy no mercy. I could do nothing, but hold on to his neck as he dog fucked me like a nasty bitch.

All around me I could smell his sweat and light cologne as he went in and out of me with force. The dick is good and hard, but I am astounded how I am taking it so well; although, I know I am going to feel it when I get home because of the way he is fucking me. I had to hold my mouth close, so I wouldn't bite my tongue from the rough ride I was on. Coby fucked me so fast and hard that he threw me on the bed and got on top of me.

Out the corner of my eye, I saw Darren jump out the way. He stood up, cheering, "Look at that bitch take that dick! That's a mother fucking solider, Coby! She acting like you ain't doing shit to her hoe ass!"

The more Darren talked down on the way I was letting him fuck me the harder Coby forced his mule dick in me. I knew he gave it to me rough and doing his best to make himself look good and me look bad. I assumed they thought I was like the regular bitches they would tag team, but I have proven them wrong. Little did they know I was taking the dick pretty good standing up, but to have it in me while I'm on my back was another story.

The way he entered me made me want to cry out for I was in mere pain because my pussy wasn't used to that type of fucking. I tried to hold on, but he was more powerful inside me in this position. Never would I want to fuck another big dick man again. That man fucked me so long and so hard that I got dry, and then wet again. He was rock hard and still going after about twenty minutes. I heard Darren call out, "You got to nut so I can get some brain. Shit yo ass being greedy with the bitch."

Normally, I would not want to be called a bitch, but good girls don't fuck like I fucked on the first night. In their eyes, I was a bitch and for that night I would be the bitch. I began moving my body a little, and Darren said, "Punish the bitch! She fucking you man!"

All I heard was Coby's chant, "Pussy too good. Pussy too good. Pussy too good."

When he spoke the last chant, he had a hard orgasm as he smashed me in the bed with all his capacity. He was grinding me like a master tool painter priming down a car before painting. He emptied a lot of nut in me because I could feel it. He slid out of me, and I could feel all his seed running out of me like an over flowing glass. Coby said, "The way you took this dick, I got to eat the pussy."

Yes, he did the unthinkable. Coby eased began my legs to eat my pussy with his nut in me doing a reverse. If he was making up for the jagged sex, he was doing a good job. My pussy was really aching and numb from his rugged fucking. She needed the smooth attention he give her. No one has fucked her like that ever. No one ever would; although, I liked getting fucked in unfamiliar styles and ways.

Bringing me back to the point of ecstasy, his tongue made me dripping wet and it didn't take long for me to cum like never before. Coby made me high as he did not stop when my orgasm started. He continued to lick on me and make my pussy scream at him for making her feel as good as she was. Darren got mad, and spoke, "Damn, Coby. You still greedy with the bitch. We supposed to sharing her, but yo ass acting like she all yours."

266

Coby did not stop eating my pussy. He did not listen to his friend. All I heard was Darren leaving out the door. I really let go and let Coby eat the hell out of my pussy. I made her bud out at him as he aimed to please. My legs could not move as I had no choice in the way he was sucking, licking, and tugging on my enlarged pussy lips. With one out cry my body shook like it was having convulsions. He got up and wiped his mouth using his hand.

The well-trained man towered over me, and spoke as he looked at me with envy, "I can get used to fucking you. Here's my number. Call me anytime you need a licking or a sticking. I ain't lying, call me!"

He put his clothes on and left me lying on the bed pleased and sore.

CHAPTER 15

I laid there staring at the ceiling. This night was the first night I have done something like that, and I got carried away. The three-some was awesome and I began to see what casual sex was all about. I was in a nut shell, understanding Henry's point of view on fucking who you want and when you want with no strings attached.

It was great liberty to get your pussy ate by who you want and take dick to the head as if it were the last piece of muscle on the planet. I was sort of shocked at myself for going hard and strong on the first night. The men were both pleased at the way I let my body be the island they were adventuring on. They each had something I enjoyed and the feel of Coby's dick in my mouth was almost as grand as Henry's, but only close.

There's something about the curve I thought with deeply smile as I finally got strength to sit up. Before I could get off the bed, Coby came in. He smiled at me, and I asked, "What is it? You lost some nut, and you want it back."

"After the way you pleased me, I want you to have some more."

"I have to go unless you can make having to go a reason to stay," I spoke quickly. Although, it was really good, but I had to go.

"Ya girl downstairs, sitting on a stool at the bar. She done fucked half the club tonight."

"Oh, she did? Because I knew two she didn't get a chance to drink up."

He walked over and touched my breast. His touch made me want some more of the good stuff he had. Coby stepped back, and said, "Every time Tongue Tammy comes here she lets mother fuckers train her ass and that's why we never fucked off with her. You don't want to first night a bitch and she has first night all the men in the club."

"No, you don't, but you didn't know me," I replied with humor.

"No, but Darren does. He picks the select few and you were one of the best of the ones I have had in a long time. Just thinking about that shit, you did make my dick hard."

I laughed as laid back down on the bed to open my legs up. He used his thumb to enter me. I became ice meeting a flame. He moved back and I sat up to put his thumb in my mouth. I sucked it while staring at him. Coby removed his thumb from me, as I said, "I have your number."

"Please use it. I won't bring a friend. I'm going to want you all by myself."

269

"You might not be able to handle me all by yourself. You might need some help."

"I might, but I don't mind finding out."

He left out. I smiled as I got dressed and made my way to see Tammy. She was where he said she was. I went over and bump her. She stared at me with displeasure, and said, "Lets' go."

I followed behind her, and asked as we saw her truck in sight, "Are you in shape to drive or do I have to?"

"I can do it. From the looks of it. You don't need to drive."

We laughed about it as we got in the truck. It is four thirty in the morning and I was hungry and sore, but satisfied. Tammy acted funny toward me, but it didn't matter. I fucked and sucked like a young prostitute fresh out of jail. I was in another world until I heard Tammy ask, "Who got into you tonight?"

"Who or what?" I asked to be funny.

"Both?"

"I went upstairs and rested."

"You rest at the house. What else you do?"

"I didn't do anything you didn't do, Tongue Tammy."

I laughed and spoke, "I didn't know they call you Tongue Tammy?"

"There's a lot of shit you don't know about when it comes to the streets."

"A lot of shit, like what?" I questioned with boldness.

"Girl, who you were with tonight?

"Girl who you were with tonight?" I asked her back.

"Cute, but be for real."

"The owner and one of his partners."

Her breath in her chest made her lungs move up and down in a fast pace. I questioned her in a nice way, "You're breathing like you mad."

"I'm good."

"What you good about? I know I'm damn good."

Those words didn't fall to the ground as she almost screamed out, "I been trying to fuck him for a minute. How the hell you get the dick before me?"

So, the bitch was trying to play my knowledge. I came right back with, "I had no idea you was trying to fuck anyone other than those you see on a daily basis."

"I fuck who I want. I was just slow this time and you fucked the dick I been wanting. Do you know how long I been after that dick?"

"Which dick you talking about, Coby or Darren?"

"Bitch you fucked both of'em!" she exclaimed as she looked from me to the road.

"What you can't believe one wanted me or both wanted me?"

"I can't believe you got, either. I been scoping out Darren and from what I hear he don't fuck with just anyone and I had planned to be the bitch he takes upstairs."

"It was nice upstairs, but Darren doesn't take just anyone upstairs."

"How the fuck you know that and this yo first time here?"

"I was told by him. We had conversations and I liked it."

"You really did fuck him?" she questioned me in a stunned way.

To open up her eyes at shit I said calmly, "I really did let them fuck me and for the record, Coby was so much better."

"And you really fucked Coby, too?"

"Yes. I got that dick. Now I know why he doesn't give it to just anyone."

"I hear the dick off the chain. I just can't believe someone like you fucked them before me."

"You mean to say how you can't believe how a pro like you lost out to a slow mover like me?"

"I got to get the dick now. I can't just let you beat me."

272

"Who is competing? I'm not, but you seem to make it a habit of fucking what I get."

She did not say another word to me as we drove a few more minutes. I know her. She is thinking about what I said. I would occasionally smile when I saw her glaring at me out the corner of my eye. We weren't ten minutes from home when she spoke, "I heard Coby dick ain't shit. I heard he is a small dick bastard and by that I don't think he can handle me anyway. I'm glad you wasted your time."

"You must be talking about the wrong Coby because the Coby I had tonight put me all against the wall and threw me on the bed, fucking the shit out of me in the air. This Coby has a mule type of dick that makes you feel every inch of him. Even when he pulls out after the nut. I guess you talking about the wrong Coby because this Coby has good dick."

She was quiet and she was mad, and I don't know for what. I spoke out, "He even gave me his personal number for me to call him when I need some more dick."

"He gave you his number?"

"Yes. He gave me his number and told Darren how good it was to him and how it was the shit. He claims he wants me to come back, but I don't know."

"You? You married hardly fucking ass is the shit?"

"Yup. That is what he said. I just couldn't believe it."

"Shit I can't believe it, but I see there is a lot you don't know."

"Please tell. I am grown and so are you. There's nothing between us but air."

"Never mind I don't want yo ass crying over shit you can't change."

"You're talking about Cedric now?"

"Fuck him! With his non-fucking ass!"

"How do you know his ass can't fuck, unless you done fucked him?" I asked her. She didn't say a word until we pulled in the driveway. I got out and went to her side. She got out the truck, and I asked her again with more emphasis, "How do you know his ass can't fuck, unless you've fucked him?"

Tammy just stood there, standing sober as I told her, "He already told me about the swinging and how he didn't want you anymore. I'm just waiting to hear it from you. Since you grown and all." Her mouth fell open as I continued, "That's right. He told me all about it. Now I want to hear it from you. Tell it all and don't leave anything covered up."

The door of her house closed and it was Jenna. I looked over at her, and she said, "Tell her Tammy, so you can come in and lick my ass. Her ass wants to know. Fuck the dumb shit let the bitch in on it. She might want to willingly participate."

Tammy began to talk like she was the shit when she spoke, "Yeah, we were fucking as swingers before you, with you and after you. Henry fucks better than he does."

If she wanted to throw a punch that carried a blow, she just did. What the hell was I thinking? She my girl and my voice of reason, but she will get down and fuck anybody. In a moment, I replied with a question of unbelief, "You fucked Henry?"

"Yo ass act like Henry is your dick? Hell, Cedric and I been swinging for years. Hell, I had both dicks before you knew what good dick was until Cedric saw you one night and wanted you. I told him you don't swing but he can try. Hell, he fell for you. I wanted you to meet Henry not Cedric, but hell it is what it is. Back to Henry and that day you came in my room, bitch you act like a motherfucker in my bed just goes to sleep. I done fucked and sucked the dicks plenty of times and some of the times, while you were in the bed resting and couldn't do a damn thang. Why else do you think he didn't nag you about fucking? Hell, he was fucking and eating this pussy like it was the greatest thing ever. You got to eat and or fuck Tammy first before you go to sleep in my bed. Hell, you got to earn your sleep in my bed, ask both

275

them. They can tell you better than I can since Cedric wants to do it like that."

In a blank in my tone of hatred I asked, "Why did you try introducing me to a man you were fucking off with. Although, you knew about the shit I had been through with Cedric and how I was feeling Henry?"

"Instead of telling you, I showed you. Ange, Henry was no good. I didn't show you Cedric he did that all on his own and you deserve the best," she said as if it were ok for her to do what she did to me.

"You think you did me a favor by fucking Henry after I met him and being with Cedric?"

"I said you deserve the best. Shit me sucking his dick and he eating my pussy did wonders for me that night because his ass can eat pussy." Tammy was almost picking at me as she spoke, and grinned, "With his long curvy dick and now that dick was good! You are missing out if you hadn't had it. Wait had it."

"Bitch you gonna pull me out of retirement just because of what you think you doing. You don't think I can see through you? You only there for someone just so you can say you did this and that for them. Once the purpose is over and the need is met, you treat people like they shit. Why else do you think you are alone? You think being known as a good time girl is the best girl in the world but it's not." My voice of reason kind of smirked as she replied with passion in front of Jenna, "You just fucked two mother fuckers you don't know so how the hell you talking about me? I'm astounded right now you can see past Cedric with his lame ass."

I walked closer upon her, and asked, "You mad because they preferred me or you super mad because the dick you want, wants me?"

Tammy was showing me a side of her that did something to my mind as she blared out, "Why the hell would I be mad? You ass ain't got shit. You ass can't even hold a job or take care of your girls. Have I asked you for shit? No! All you have to do was stay in my bed and let me eat and fuck you. That's it! You can't see I'm the best for you. Fuck those other motherfuckers. They ain't got shit, but real dick and horse tongues. You would never worry about shit, but pleasing me, but you act like you can't take hints. I have wanted to eat your pussy since you moved in and when I got it, I claimed it. Henry was mad because I was being greedy tongue fucking you, but hell he should have done it right when he had you on the balcony."

I wanted to faint. I never knew how she felt about me. She spoke more, "Jenna and I listened at him pleasing you. I actually got turned on and fucked the shit of her. How are you tripping, anyway? I am in my own damn house and not in yours. Oops my bad, your sorry excuse of a husband fucked up the insurance money, and now you living on me and won't live with me. Bitch, you need to shut the fuck up and let me do me."

"Doing you does not mean doing me. I don't want a damn woman."

"Your pussy tasted real good and I ain't lying. Your juices were sweet, and I can still smell you. The tongue is a muscle that please bitches and niggas and with your eyes closed you won't even know if it's a man or a woman."

"I can't believe what I am hearing right now. You been after me the whole time? You were playing me and my situation for your advantage just so you can get me to swing with you?"

"Hell yeah! I wanted you for me and if that meant doing what I did, I do it again because I'm that bitch who has it going on."

"How the hell you talking when you don't even talk to your child? You lounge around screwing anything that moves."

"That includes you? If my memory serves me correctly, I fucked Henry all night after I ate your pussy while you were drunk. Hell, I woke up with bad breath."

"That's because what's in you come out of you and if your breath stank, then, your stanking ass pussy has gingivitis."

"So, me letting you throw your pussy in my mouth wasn't nothing?"

My mouth flew open as I walked off some. She said, "What can you say? I ate your pussy, bad breath and all. You let a bi-sexual life coach bitch drink your nut. Now, you woke and all worked up, let me and Jenna take care of your way. You should give me some type of pay back after all I have done for you and those damn kids. Hell, you would still be in the hotel if I hadn't done you a favor and had a heart by putting up with you."

"Earlier there wasn't anything between us, but air and now opportunity," I stated back as I hit her with all my might in the face. Tammy staggered back against the truck as Jenna stood there watching. I hit Tammy again as she clawed at me. She tried scratching my face. I was no match for her as she hit me a few more times. I fell on the ground. Tammy got on top of me. She was hitting me in the head as I swung back. Somehow, I discovered strength and threw her off me.

Tammy laughed as I rolled under her truck to the other side. Jenna came over, and Tammy said, "This bitch done blown my high. What you got in there to settle me down?"

"I can give you a little closed for business sex, since you been fighting."

They laughed as Tammy was walking off she started falling because I snatched her feet from under her. Jenna hollered out, "What the hell!"

I came from under the truck with hatred. I emerged as a bitter woman who has been fighting an incredible battle and just now realizing it. I had so much built up inside me that losing was not going to happen. I can't believe the one person I trusted with my life was vicious for not being in my life. I am no dyke or selfish, but enough is enough. It hurts to know how she deliberately sabotaged my relationship because she wanted me.

Nothing hurts more than knowing the person you trusted was the real snake. Tammy disguised herself extremely well and had me fooled. She is FAM and for her to stoop so low was farfetched. She and I have never fought and for us to do this at a time in our lives was not needed. There was nothing I would do for her and for her to be like this to me was heartbreaking.

The word bitch came to mind when she fell face first. Quickly I got from under the truck and pushed Jenna down. I straddled Tammy and Jenna screamed, "Get the fuck off her, bitch!" while jumping on my back. I threw her off.

She hit the ground hard and moaned. I continued my attack on Tammy. I don't believe anyone could stop me from hurting her. She had done so much to help me and yet so much to hurt me. I hadn't realized how blank I was until I heard her moan. I scanned her face and saw she was indeed bloody with half closed eyes.

It is here I hit her one last time in the face before letting her fall to the ground. Jenna was sitting up. I went over to her and punched her in the face when I said, "The next time you touch me I will make sure you don't touch me again!"

She didn't answer as she went over to Tammy. I snatched my purse off the ground and went in the house to my hidden spot. I had a lot of cash saved, but I took two hundred dollars. Soon as my feet touched the last step Jemma was a crutch for Tammy. I spoke with attitude and anger, "Since you can't afford respect for me or yourself, here's two hundred dollars, buy you some.

I tore up the money in my hand in small pieces and threw it at her. Tammy was bawling and reaching for me. She has no idea how distraught I am. It actually made me sick to know how trusting I was and how she took it lightly. In reality she was no better than Henry or Cedric. She was worse because she was family, and I treated her with loyalty but not anymore.

CHAPTER 16

I walked until I couldn't walk anymore. I ended up at the park. I sat on the bench and cried. It really hurts about Tammy. I could not avoid it. I begin to think how *she would dress sexually for Henry's attention and do inappropriate things when Cedric was there. She didn't want to be left out. She would put me down in her own sneaky way and I wouldn't say anything. There had been conversations where I would evade any questions or remarks she would make. Nevertheless, she had no right to disrespect me on any level.*

I thought of Henry as something more. *I wanted him to be something more. I knew he was a friend, which turned into something more.* I thought about the question, *why didn't he tell me? I could not grasp my mind around him and her or her and Cedric. He hurt me without knowing how important he was. I listened to him over Tammy because he made sense as well as understood my point of view. I was easy and looking for a real friend, but that wasn't it.*

I've confused friendship over hearing the voices of reason. The evidence was right in front of me and I refused it. How could I have been so naïve about the life these Boss Players lived? They do this shit for a living. I was a beginner in the hoe world who didn't think of being taken in by those in my life. It was a red flag when Henry stated he could never love me like he should because he didn't believe in love.

Cedric started a ripple effect. He put things in motion and I should thank him. But, Vesta Kelly said it best by saying, "Snowflakes are one of nature's most fragile things, but just look at what they can do when they stick together." That was not a lie. The three of them stuck together and stuck it to me. They all kept me in the dark about their secret life. I wouldn't have wanted in on the swinging, but they each should have told me.

If I hadn't heard Cedric call out Tam or if I hadn't read the text message, I might still be in the dark. I didn't go back to her house. I would buy my girls new clothes and live somewhere temporarily, but not there. I tried drying my face, but the tears wouldn't stop. Being hurt by three people was far worse than being hurt by one.

I spoke loud enough for me to hear, "Lord I was gullible for them to take me through the ringer? Lord I only wanted happiness. Tammy above all was my confidant. I didn't lead her on. I am hurt and angry for the way my life has turned out. If someone had put this treachery of my life in a movie. I still wouldn't believe it, but it's true. My voices of reason did more heartache and turmoil than anything. I need healing. I need your help. I pray my place is ready soon. My children and I are homeless again. I only have you. Amen."

I would be lying if I said I felt better. It should sink in how trusting I was to people that didn't have my best interest. My cell rang and it was Cedric. I pushed ignore for he is still my husband and that made it no better. He and Tammy showed their love hate relationship to the fullest and I bought it. My cell rang again and it was Cedric. I cleared my voice and spoke, "Hello."

"Tammy called me."

"I am not in the mood right now."

"I know, but where you? I can come get you."

"I don't need you to come get me."

"Where are you going to stay? You do have to think about the girls."

"Cedric all I have ever thought about was the girls."

"You aren't thinking about them now."

"I am. I won't confuse them about us. I would rather stay in a hotel."

"You want Lyn, don't you?"

"Yes, I do!" I screamed.

"Well get a place if you don't I will split the girls up because you being stupid right now."

"You see I just became homeless for the second time in my life, and you are not concerned about that, either."

"I am concerned. Why you think I want you here with me?"

"I won't stay with you, and things will get better as the day goes. I will call you back with an answer."

"Ok. I look forward in hearing from you."

I hung up and prayed I hear from Mrs. Waters; although, it should be another two weeks. I continued sitting in my wet clothes and a purse full of money. I wish I hadn't torn up that money and threw it at her, but I did. I had to pick up the girls, but I don't have a ride. I sat there and thought about Henry. Now would be the perfect time to use him. I called him and he told me he would come get me. I thought about calling Mrs. Waters and my cell rung. I looked at it and saw it Mrs. Waters. My heart began to beat rapidly as she said, "I hope I am not catching you at a bad time."

"Your timing is perfect. I was just thinking about you."

"I hope good thoughts" she said with a cheer.

"It was. Nothing is wrong is it?" I asked.

"Aw no. Everything is perfect I was calling about you moving in early?"

Tears stroll down my face. I was homeless with nowhere to go but back to the people who has all hurt me. I heard her say, "You there?"

"Yes" I spoke through my tears.

"Are you crying, dear?"

"I am crying tears of joy. I prayed about you calling me and here you are calling me. I know sometimes what we want doesn't come as fast but mine did. I thank you for calling me. Would it be ok if I brought you the money today; although, I know today is Sunday?"

"Can you bring it on Monday? I am actually on my way back and I am exhausted."

"Early Monday morning will be fine."

"Great that way we can go over to the lawyer's office to have the paperwork recorded through him."

"Thanks so much, Mrs. Waters."

"Your welcome dear."

We hung up and Henry was standing there. He sat down, and I exclaimed, "The house is ready, and I'll be able to move in it tomorrow."

"I am so glad."

"I know me, too."

"You need me to take you there or you gonna get Tammy?"

I gave him a blank stare as I spoke, "I guess you haven't heard."

"Heard what?"

"Tammy and I were fighting this morning."

"For real? Fist fighting?"

"Yeah. If you didn't know, how did you know to find me at the park?"

"I don't live far from here remember and sometimes I come here before church service."

"Oh. I'm sorry. You do live walking distance."

"No problem."

We weren't saying anything for a moment. I faced him, and spoke out, "Please tell me about you, Tammy and Cedric."

"There isn't much worth speaking on."

"Rewind. Tell me about the life of you, Tammy, Cedric, and Emma before the three of you met me."

He kind of grinned as he replied, "Oh that life."

"Yes that life."

"How do you know, if you know anything?"

"If I didn't know I wouldn't be asking, but to put things in faster motion, Cedric and Tammy told me of their life. I need to hear about you."

"You sure?"

"Yes. You know all about me. You know that Tammy ate my pussy that night I was drunk."

"I do."

"You also know I don't swing."

"I do."

I turned my head away from his face. He said, "When Tammy was at her old place, we all were swingers. My cousin introduced Tammy to the swinging lifestyle, and she met Emma. When I met Emma, she introduced me to a girl she was seeing, which happened to be Tammy."

"Where do I fit in all this?"

"One night you called Tammy and told her you were outside. We all hid in her room. You came in and I saw you while I was peeping through the door. Cedric didn't see you then, but anyway. I liked you. I told Tammy to hook me up, but she told me you don't swing and that made me like you more. I was to meet you, but my car broke down and Cedric accidentally met you so I backed off. When we really did meet, I still wanted you."

He spoke to my heart, "You are what we call safe. But, with you I want chances, and those chances could mean my heart. I can't have that, Angela. I never had what you call real love. For a man in your life it has to be the best thing or so damn close you can't tell it. I refuse being caught up and strung out in love."

"Real love exists because God is love."

"Only in the movies and at that they get paid to pretend."

"Love is real and I believe in it. I will not let how Cedric did me make love look bleak and hopeless because it is not."

We left the park without saying another word. Before getting the girls, we went to Dollar General for a few clothes and personal items. I thanked him as we headed for my loves and he replied, "Anything for a real friend."

We arrived where the girls were. I went in and got them. Henry took us to a hotel. I picked out a cheap one, but he paid for an expensive one for two days. I politely thank him as we went in the room. The girls put on cartoons as usual while I look at the window. When time started winding down, I ordered a medium pizza, a 2-liter of coke with regular wings. We ate and cleaned up the table. The girls bathed and went to sleep. I text Cedric and told him I will most definitely call him tomorrow and he texted the letter K. I took a bath and slept in peace.

The next morning, I woke fresh and happy. I mean real joy. I felt that my prayers were answered. I called Mrs. Waters and asked what would be a good time and she stated within the next hour. I called Henry and asked if he could take me by the lawyer's office in thirty minutes. He said yes and I was obliged. We got ready and Lyn was looking out the window when she saw Henry pull up. She started jumping up and down. I knew it had to be him.

Her joy made me smile I just hate it's not the joy she needs towards another man. I grabbed my purse as Lyn got her and her sister's bag. I locked the door and we all got in the car. I was thoughtless at the fact that I hadn't taken their seats out of Henry's car. I saw them, and he spoke, "Yes. They been in here for a while."

I laughed as we took off to the lawyer's office. When we got there, I saw Mrs. Waters, and she had a delightful smile. Henry waited in the waiting room with the girls while I handled business. The lawyer explained about the payments coming to his office and the deed will be mine when the last payment is paid. Mrs. Waters already had the utilities turned on. I didn't even know how she did it, but she says she knows people in places and that was enough for me.

I even loved how she had it set up that if anything happens to her, no one can take the home from me, but I can lose it if I don't pay, which was understandable. I signed the papers, paid the money, and got the keys. I cried. I have done something on my own and I didn't have Cedric or Tammy's help. Soon as I walked out the office, Henry saw my face and shook his head for approval. I handed Henry the hotel key for him to return it. I picked up Rossi, and said, "Lets' go to our new home."

"We stay Aunt Tammy's?"

"No, we have our own place now."

"The swing?" Lyn asked.

"Yes, the one with the swing."

"Yay!" she yelled, and Rossi did what she did.

We locked the girls down and headed to my home. When we got there, we saw the grass was cut and it was more gorgeous than before. I put my hands in my face and cried. I am a homeowner and it's really hitting me that I did it, not Cedric, but me. Little ole me having the blessing of God showing up for me made me cry more. I heard Lyn ask, "Is mommy crying?"

"Mommy crying?" Rossi spoke.

"She's happy," Henry said to comfort the girls.

"Happy tears?" Lyn said.

"Happy tears" Rossi said.

Henry spoke, "You can cry when you are happy."

"Oh. Can we swing now?" Lyn asked.

I dried my face, and spoke, "Go on I have to call C-e-d-r-i-c."

"Ok," Henry said as he unlocked the girls.

They all ran towards the swings as I dialed Cedric. He picked up, and said, "You ready to talk?"

"I am calling you to tell you a few songs. Please hear me out with no interruptions."

"Ok. What songs?"

"Rhianna song says, Take a Bow and you should. Beyoncé song says, Drunk in Love because I was like a dog chasing its tail and jumping through hoops for you. Chris Brown song says, Say Goodbye and I am. But, when you add Usher song Papers, you'll get R. Kelly telling me, You Deserve Better and I do, therefore, K. Michelle two song says, You Can't Raise A Man and Kiss My Ass. If you want to talk, talk through my lawyer. From this day forward we have nothing to discuss."

I hung up on him and felt better. I had enough. As long as I keep hearing him whisper tender nothings I would forever be going around in circles. He called me back, but I didn't answer. I put him on the block list. I got out and went in my very own house. The girls came in with Henry and Lyn said, "My room, Rossi."

We followed behind the girls and they each have a room across from the other while mine is down the hall to the other side. The house is really beautiful, and I needed furniture. Henry told me I could go sign up for furniture and etc., at the local church. I must have proof of income and the girl's birth certificates. We locked up and he took me to the church and within the next hour I had a bump bed set, a king size bed, a kitchen dinette table set, and a couch.

I knew that was really the Lord working on my behalf and I cried. I was so emotional and praising God for this happy outcome in my life. I vowed to go back to church and pay tithes. I like Henry's church, but I won't go there because he will be there. I will find another place, until then, we will watch Jimmy Swaggart for all our services. We will even get dressed and participate as they do. Distracting me was Henry. He stood in front of me, and said, "What you thinking about?"

"How the Lord has blessed someone like me who doesn't deserve HIS grace and mercy, but HE gave it anyway."

"HE gave it because HE is not an unrighteous God. I have to go, but I will come by and check on you if that is ok?"

"That'll be fine. The next thing I get is a car. I won't keep you chauffeuring me around."

"I don't mind."

"I know you don't, but I do."

"Angela, whenever you need me, I am just a phone call, or a text away. Please call me. I know we can't make what you want a reality, but this is as close as it gets for me. Love won't catch me off guard."

"That makes me sad because I feel we could have something special, but our lives and our beliefs are different. You love Jimmy while I love T. D. Jakes, and you don't believe in women preaching."

"Let me change that up. I mean I don't believe in women preaching that don't have her head covered by sitting under a man speaker."

"You and your beliefs get out my house," I spoke with funniness.

"Well we are just that different and opposite do attract."

"They do, but not us."

"Bye, Angela."

"Bye, Henry."

CHAPTER 17

"WHERE THE FUCK IS MY PERIOD!" I screamed loudly. I don't remember the last time she was around. I knew if I am pregnant has to be Cedric's. I fucked Coby and Darren with condoms. I felt numb as I thought *of another child.* I am barely getting by, and another baby would be something serious. *"I could*n*'t be pregnant,"* I said to myself. *I knew how I will do this if that be the case, but for right now, that was not the issue.* I closed my thoughts and went to bed.

The next morning, I called a cab and looked for Head start that accepts four-year old and a waiting list for Rossi. In the meantime, I will teach her what I knew. Between me and educational channels she will learn. For a special treat I took the girls out. We enjoyed our day until I saw Cedric. He was with Emma. They saw me and I made sure the girls didn't see them as we left. I felt hurt all over again.

I can't keep doing this. The longer I show him I care the more he will think he has the upper hand I thought as I saw a text. It was from my lawyer. I opened it and read: Court on Friday at nine thirty a.m. I swallowed and paid for the cab fare when we got out. We had a few bags, and we took them in the house. I cooked a small dinner for us. The next thing I know I heard a horn blow. I saw it was Cedric. He was alone, but that mattered not. I don't want to see him, but went outside, anyway. He got out the car and stood at his car as he said, "Can we talk?"

"I thought I told you to talk through my lawyer?"

"I am, but today when I saw how happy you and the girls were, I decided to let Lyn stay with you. I can't take her away from you and Rossi. You guys are the only family she knows. I love her, but you are a great mother to her, and I thank you for that. I had women before you and Lyn was always getting attached. She was calling them momma, and it wasn't right. None of that counted until I met and married you. I just want to thank you Angela for being an outstanding mom. I want visitations once a month and on birthdays. Emma or whoever I have in my life won't come around them during these visits unless you say so. I already told my lawyer this and now I am telling you. I regret hurting you and I regret how we turned out, but we can't change it."

He blew my mind. I walked over to him, and said, "Thank you from the bottom of my heart for letting Lyn stay with me. She is mine she has always been mine."

"I know. We saw you first and we just stood by watching how you were with them. You are genuinely a mother."

"Thank you, Cedric. I never thought we would be having this conversation."

"I know and you didn't even ask about Emma.'

"I am better about that. You have gone on with your life and I will do the same thing."

I gave him a hug. I moved back from him and smiled as I walked off from him and went back in where the girls were as if he never came by. It felt good to feel strong enough to tell him how I felt and not clam up or feel a certain way when he was around. I was better about it, and I applaud myself for that. However, the time came for my court. I text Henry to remind him about taking me and he responded by saying he was on his way.

I checked my time again and saw that it was too early. I don't have to be there until two and a half hours from now. Seconds later he pulled up and I went to the door for him to get out. He did. I closed the door and when he walked in I asked, "Would you like some coffee?"

"No thank you."

"Grab a seat."

He sat at the end of the couch, and I sat at the other. He said, "I know you it's nine thirty, but we need to talk."

"About what?"

"About Tammy."

I did a major sigh as he called her name. I hadn't thought about her second to none since that night and here he is bringing her in to me. I spoke, "Why you want me to talk about her?"

"I just don't want you to talk about her. I want y'all to talk."

"Fuck that bitch! I couldn't believe the way she was with me. She ate my pussy while I was drunk. I thought it was you because of what we just shared. It disgusts me to know she was pleasing me. Don't you know she thinks she is the best for me? My own fucking blood."

"She is fam, Angela."

"Fuck fam! Look what she did!"

"You don't mean that. You are still hurt."

"Like hell I do. She intentionally tried destroying me for personal gain. She was fucking my husband before me; swinging style and never told me. Again, I repeat she got me drunk and ate my pussy. Now you tell me about the love of fam?"

Henry says, "William Shedd stated how a ship in a harbor is safe, but that is not what ships are built for."

I listened as he said gracefully, "And, neither are you Angela. You are meant to be out there among the people showing your radiant smile and being a wonderful mother. You are better than this. You can't harbor ill feelings they will take root like a tree and grow into something bigger. I am humbly sorry for my part in the pain. I never meant to hurt you and that is the God knows truth. I developed infatuation feelings towards you the more I hung out with you. I've talked intimately with you and you are a part of my life in your own way. I would think about you, but I couldn't let you know how thoughts of you were consuming me. You are a married woman and at that time I was a married man, too. You will always be important if you never see me or talk to me again. In so many ways you are my voice of reason; therefore, listen. Talk to Tammy. You would give me sound advice and sometimes I found myself listening to your plain ole ways. You made sense and that night we were together, we made sense."

The air between he and I was calm and more relaxed. He touched my hand and said, "You hear anything I said from my heart?"

"I heard you and I do forgive you. We won't be like we were."

"I know we won't, but as long as we still talk and have no secrets. I'm ok with that, but what about Tammy?"

"I will call her right now in front of you because after today I am so done."

He used his cell and dialed Tammy. She answered the phone in a crying way as she spoke, "What do you want, Henry?"

"Angela is here, and I have convinced her to talk to you."

"Ange, you there for real?"

"Yes, Tammy, what is it?"

"I am so sorry for all I did. Won't you and the girls come back and let me make it up. I have missed you all."

"Thanks, but no thanks. We have a place of our own."

"That's good."

I looked at Henry and he kind of humped his shoulders as I asked, "Is there anything else, Tammy?"

"Just want to say I didn't mean to fuck things up between us. You were there for me when I had no one in my life and I can't believe I fell for you like that. You my FAM and I fucked you big time. I took advantage of you and I am paying the cost now for that."

"I forgive you, but not ready to see or be around you just yet. All that will take some time, but I'm sure we'll be talking again, but not ever like before."

"I am just happy you are talking mow."

"Thank, Henry, for that."

"I thank God, too, because I know if HE hadn't touched your heart there would be no way in this earth you will be as friendly towards me like you are."

"Alright. Later, Tammy."

"Bye, Ange."

I hung up, and spoke, "Was that to your liking?"

"It's not my liking. It's about how you feel?"

"I'm ok. I guess it's out the way and over with. I don't have to worry about doing it later."

"Let me get the girls up."

"We can eat breakfast before you go in court."

"You can take them while I am inside. I am not hungry, just nervous."

"What about?"

"Good question. I talked to Cedric, and he was with Emma."

"Oh really?"

"Yes. He came over and told me he was giving me custody of Lyn with supervised supervisions."

"That is great news, Angela."

"I know. Let me get the girls up so we can make it official."

I went to get the girls up and we locked them down. Lyn was happy as always to see Henry and I hate he has become a major factor in her life. They dropped me off and left. I went inside and I didn't see Cedric. I saw Emma. She was walking my way when she got to me she said, "Cedric won't be here today, but he told the lawyer to go on and give you whatever you wanted."

"What's wrong with Cedric?"

"He was shot last night."

"Is he ok?"

"He is doing better."

"Why wasn't I notified? I am the wife."

"He said he didn't want you worried or coming to see him. You have the girls, and he did not want you to drag them in the night air."

My lawyer appeared through the door saying, "We ready."

I went in behind him and didn't remember anything. My focus was on Cedric and hoping he was really ok. I snapped out of it when the judge hit the gavel, and my lawyer said, "You got everything you asked for but you are still legally married until he can come in and sign."

I texted Henry and told him to come on. He arrived and I left headed to the hospital. Henry watched the girls as I went in to see Cedric. He saw me and tried sitting up. I shook my head no and he became still. I sat next to him, and he asked, "Are we divorced yet?"

"No. You have to get well and sign it."

"Oh" he said in a sad tone.

"How are you feeling? You done got yourself shot to stop the divorce," I spoke to make him smile and he did.

"Nah I tried to get killed so you will still be my wife, and I would be able to take care of you for life."

"That is not funny, Cedric. I do not want you dead. It would hurt me too much if something happens to you."

"I know, but it sounded good didn't it."

"Yes, it did," I spoke as I touched his hand.

He gave me a look like no other and I didn't like it. He said, "I love you Angela after all I had done to you. I'm glad we still married, and I am glad to see your beautiful face and that smile that melts my heart."

"You always know what to say."

"You still my wife and I know you will come especially now when I needed you the most. Emma knows I have never stopped loving you and she was just a good time girl."

"As long as you are alive and those papers are not signed, I am your wife. Why you talking, anyway? Get your rest and get out the hospital. The girls want to show you their swing and their tree house out back."

"I am glad you got the house. They have a tree house, too?"

"Yes, and you need to come by and see it. The house is more beautiful on the inside."

"Anywhere you are at, it's beautiful. You make things better."

I leaned up and kissed his forehead. He said, "You have always smelled nice. I used to go to work at the school thinking about how sweet you smelled and how fabulous you looked being a superwoman to me and the girls. I have always been so proud of you, and I never really told you. I guess I was being selfish and thinking about self."

"You were, weren't you" and we laughed. Then I said,

"All that happened, supposed to have happened because it was to happened. I am living in the right now. NOW, get yourself better and where did they shoot you at?"

"I was shot in the stomach, and it hurts like hell" he spoke with a tense face.

"Have you prayed to God for saving you because it could have been worse?"

"I know and no. Pray with me and for me."

This is a first I thought as I said, "Lord we ask that you forgive Cedric of his sins and work on his heart as he lay in this bed. I know YOU love him because I love him. We ask for YOUR Will Lord and not what we want. We know YOU can do anything and healing is a small thing compared to all YOU can do. We thank you and we appreciate YOU, in Jesus name."

We both said, "Amen" but Cedric wouldn't let go of my hand as he said, "Lord I ask that I make up for the wrong I have done to this woman and my children. Allow me to make it right and keep it right. Amen."

When he finished, he spoke to my soul, "Now it's right." The way he said that gave me chills. He stared at me, and said, "Take care of my son and name him after me."

"You don't know what you are talking about."

He did not get a chance to talk further because the nurse came in, and said, "It's time for Mr. Myers to rest before he goes back into surgery."

"I will check back on you tomorrow and we can continue this discussion about a son."

"I love you so much, my charming and faithful wife," Cedric spoke in a happy way.

"I will always love you Mr. Cedric Myers. Bye, Cedric," I spoke with humor and a smile for him.

I heard him telling the nurse how he wasn't ready to go to surgery. I closed the door and went back to the waiting room and told Henry he was doing ok and talking out his neck. We locked the girls down in the car as they were all singing and carrying. We waited for a few minutes because I wanted to go back in and talk to him about what he said, but decided against it. As Henry was driving off, I saw someone running in the rear-view mirror. I yelled out, "Stop the car!"

Henry smashed on brakes and my body went forward. I got out the car and saw it was the nurse. When I stared into her stricken face, I knew he was gone. Her frantic look and the feel in my heart just knew it. Henry saw it and talked to the girls as the nurse and I talked. She shook her head in a sorrowful manner, and said, "I don't know how to tell you, but he's gone. You just left him and now he's gone."

I didn't believe her as I went inside and saw for myself. He was covered up and when I uncovered it, I saw it was indeed him. He had such a peaceful look on his face and the smile he had was one I had fallen in love with. I tried not fainting as the nurse allowed me to lean on her. *How do I tell my girls their father was gone? How do I tell my heart the love of my life was gone?* I heard no answers as I sat at his side crying.

So many emotions rushed through me as I sat there touching his hand. *We just finished praying and having a peaceful conversation. We just finished talking* I kept telling myself it was not true, but I knew better. Some of his friends came, even Tammy. She gave me a hug, and I needed that. Henry was still with the girls, and I didn't worry for he was taking good care of them as I greeted people.

The next day was the roughest. I have to plan a funeral and get everything organized. Picking out his uniform was the hardest because I would think back to him telling me how he has always wanted to be a cop like his dad was before him. We weren't together when he got the job but I knew he loved every minute of it. The Chief came by and told me how it happened. He said, a husband and wife got into a dispute, and he and his partner were sent to resolve it. When they got there, the woman was rational about them taking her husband to jail, for he had warrants.

When they read him his rights, the disturbed woman came out the house with the gun. She was aiming it at his partner, and he moved him out the way. She shot him and began shooting at the partner. He shot her and called for an ambulance. She died on the spot and Cedric will be awarded the highest Medal of Honor for a police officer to receive for his bravery. I cried because I hate he has lost his life for the award his dad got when he was older.

All I could see was Cedric's face and his smile. I did not dwell on the pain he caused me, I only thought of our last encounter. He knew he was dying. He had to have known because of the way he said "Now it's right." I had a hard time sleeping and believing he was really gone. No matter how I told myself he was gone. Even his cousins flew in and are staying at a hotel. Luckily Tammy and Henry are helping me. Lyn kind of understands but Rossi doesn't.

I knew the girls would take it hard. I debated on them going. On the other hand, I would let them view the body. I really hadn't talk to anyone because I do not trust my voice to speak. No one but God knew how I been crying at night for him. I feel that I cannot go on, but I must. Out of nowhere I felt so sick. *I have to straighten up,* I thought as laid on the bed.

The day of the funeral came and I got a phone call. It was Emma. I was waiting for Emma to come around, but she didn't. She stayed her distance and that day she called me. I answered it saying, "Hello."

"Angela, it's me, Emma." I was quiet as she said, "I am not trying to start anything, but I want you to know that he loved you and I hate what I did to you and him."

I was quiet and stunned, she had even called me. I spoke, "That is the past and he is gone. Neither I nor you can change it. If you don't mind, I have to go bury my husband."

I hung up and cried as I put on my shades. Henry came over while Tammy was getting the girls ready. He asked, "You ok?"

"I can't say right now. I am about to bury the one man I have loved more than a love for a long time."

"I know you still love him, and you were trying to get over him."

"Henry, you know what he told me before he died?"

"What he tell you?"

"To name his son after him."

"You pregnant?"

"Not that I know of."

"You better check that out."

308

"Right now, we have a funeral."

We left the house and went to the church. The girls weren't crying, but alert. I was off in another world and don't remember much of nothing, but people hugging me as they walked by. We were in the last stage of a divorce, but not divorced. I just sat there, wiping my eyes and being strong for Lyn for she understands a lot more than Rossi. Henry took Lyn out the church because she was crying for her daddy.

I walked with his family to the grave site. The police gave him a salute, and the Chief gave me the Medal of Honor on behalf of the City. I held it close to my heart as if it was going to change something, but it didn't. When the funeral was over I did a double take, and saw Coby. He was dressed in police uniform and my mouth fell open. He came over to me and I asked Henry to excuse me. Coby said, "Hi, Angela."

"Coby what you are doing here?" I stammered out.

"I was Cedric's partner."

"You? He saved your life?"

"Yeah, and him saving my life is something I can't forget."

"So, that night you knew about me?"

"I did and I didn't. He talked about you all the time and how he left a good woman for a free woman. He used to tell me how he wished he could undo his life and be a better man to you and a father to the kids."

"But, you still slept with me after knowing I was your partner's wife."

"After I got back to work, I told him how I met this woman that would be perfect except I slept with her on the first night. He said she might be a swinger. I said no. Darren picked her out and he knows like I know that Darren is particular about the women he picks out. In fact, Darren had investigated you before he picked you. So he made his move because he found out you are a good girl. Cedric said I bet you this isn't her. When he showed me your picture, I had to lie really hard by saying it wasn't you. He talked highly of you all the time. He was making me fall in love with you just by the things he was saying. You might not believe it, but you made his last days, worth it."

"Thank you, Coby, for telling me all this."

"Out of respect, will it be ok to check on you and the girls? I won't be able to live with myself if you say no. I want to be the role model for them because he's not here for them."

"You can do so."

He gave me a hug, and said, "Thank you so much."

I went in my house, and many people were there for the repast. Some I knew and some I didn't but there are there for Cedric. The girls were doing ok and playing as if nothing has happened. *I wish I could be like that,* I thought as I watched them play and enjoy life before it becomes the way it can.

One by one people were leaving and before long the girls and I were alone. I put them to bed and took the test. What do you know I'm pregnant just like he said? I cried again with mixed emotions. I know its Cedric's, but if it wasn't he died believing it was his and because of that, it was his baby and that's final.

Epilogue

Angela had a son and named him Cedric Myers Jr.

She became financially stable and lived off the Widow's Pension.

She and Henry never hooked up again. In fact, she slowly pulled away from Henry for he believed Cedric Jr. was his, but didn't contest it.

Angela and Coby eventually got married and had another son.

Tammy, Emma, and Jenna are still single swinging dykes.

www.ingramcontent.com/pod-product-compliance
Lightning Source LLC
Chambersburg PA
CBHW021457240626
47154CB00002B/416